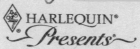

HARLEQUIN®
Presents

Don't miss out on any of our books in March!

This month, Lynne Graham brings you
The Italian Billionaire's Pregnant Bride,
the last story in her brilliant trilogy THE RICH, THE
RUTHLESS AND THE REALLY HANDSOME, where
tycoon Sergio Torrente demands that pregnant Kathy
marry him. In *The Spaniard's Pregnancy Proposal*
by Kim Lawrence, Antonio Rochas is sexy,
smoldering and won't let relationship-shy Fleur
go easily! In Trish Morey's *The Sheikh's Convenient
Virgin,* a devastatingly handsome desert prince
is in need of a convenient wife who must be pure.
Anne Mather brings you a brooding Italian who
believes Juliet is a gold-digger in *Bedded for the
Italian's Pleasure.* In *Taken by Her Greek Boss*
by Cathy Williams, Nick Papaeliou can't understand
why he's attracted to frumpy Rose—but her
shapeless garments hide a very alluring woman.
Lindsay Armstrong's *From Waif to His Wife* tells the
story of a rich businessman who avoids marriage—
but one woman's sensual spell clouds his perfect
judgment! In *The Millionaire's Convenient Bride*
by Catherine George, a dashing millionaire needs
a temporary housekeeper—but soon the business
arrangement includes a wedding! Finally, in
One-Night Love Child by Anne McAllister, Flynn
doesn't know he's the father of Sara's son—but
when he discovers the truth he *will* possess her....
Happy reading from Harlequin Presents!

MISTRESS
TO A
MILLIONAIRE

She's his in the bedroom,
but he can't buy her love…

Showered with diamonds, draped in exquisite
lingerie, whisked around the world in the lap of
luxury…

The ultimate fantasy becomes a reality.

Live the dream with more
MISTRESS TO A MILLIONAIRE titles
by your favorite authors.

Available only from Harlequin Presents®

Anne McAllister

ONE-NIGHT LOVE CHILD

MISTRESS TO A MILLIONAIRE

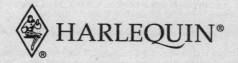

HARLEQUIN®

TORONTO • NEW YORK • LONDON
AMSTERDAM • PARIS • SYDNEY • HAMBURG
STOCKHOLM • ATHENS • TOKYO • MILAN • MADRID
PRAGUE • WARSAW • BUDAPEST • AUCKLAND

ISBN-13: 978-0-373-12714-6
ISBN-10:   0-373-12714-6

ONE-NIGHT LOVE CHILD

First North American Publication 2008.

This edition published by arrangement with Harlequin Books S.A.

www.eHarlequin.com

Printed in U.S.A.

All about the author…
Anne McAllister

RITA® Award-winning author **ANNE McALLISTER**
was born in California. She spent formative summer
vacations on the beach near her home, on her
grandparents' small ranch in Colorado and visiting
relatives in Montana. Studying the cowboys, the surfers
and the beach-volleyball players, she spent long hours
developing her concept of "the perfect hero." (Have
you noticed a lack of hard-driving type-A businessmen
among them? Well, she promises to do one soon, just
for a change!)

One thing she did do, early on, was develop a weakness
for lean, dark-haired, handsome lone-wolf-type guys.
When she finally found one, he was in the university
library where she was working. She knew a good
man when she saw one. They've now been sharing
"happily ever afters" for over thirty years. They have
four grown children and a steadily increasing number
of grandchildren. They also have three dogs who keep
her fit by taking her on long walks every day.

Quite a few years ago they moved to the Midwest, but
they spend more and more time in Montana. And as
Anne says, she lives there in her head most of the time
anyway. She wishes a small town like her very own
Elmer, Montana, existed. She'd move there in a minute.
But she loves visiting big cities as well, and New York
has always been her favorite.

Before she started writing romances, Anne taught
Spanish, capped deodorant bottles, copyedited
textbooks, got a master's degree in theology and
ghostwrote sermons. Strange and varied, perhaps,
but all grist for the writer's mill, she says.

For Anne Gracie who kept my head above water

For Nancy, Cathy and Steve
who shared the journey

And for Kimberley Young, whose editorial
comments made this a better book

CHAPTER ONE

THE letter arrived out of the blue.

"I don't know what it is, my lord." Mrs. Upham sniffed, then dangled the smudged and tattered pale-blue envelope from between two fingers with clear disapproval. "It's very... dirty."

She had put the rest of the post on Flynn's desk in neat sorted stacks as she always did. Estate business—the biggest stack. Fan mail and book business—the midsize stack. Personal letters from his mother or brother—neither of whom seemed to believe in phones or e-mail—in the third.

All very tidy and organized—as if she could do the same to Flynn's life.

Good luck, he thought.

As his life currently consisted of Dunmorey, a dank and crumbling five-hundred-odd-year-old castle full of portraits of disapproving ancestors who looked down their noses at Flynn's efforts to literally keep a roof over their heads, its attendant farms, lands and tenants, as well as his horse-mad brother, Dev, who had great plans for reviving the Dunmorey stud but no money to accomplish it, and his mother, whose mantra since his father's death seven months ago had been, "We need to find you a bride," Flynn didn't think Mrs. Upham was likely to find any joy in it at all.

The only joy he could give her would be to tell her to throw it out.

His father certainly would have.

The late eighth earl of Dunmorey had no patience for anything that wasn't proper and traditional. He had once thrown out a letter Flynn had scrawled on a piece of a paper bag from a war zone where he'd been working on a story.

"If you can't be bothered to write a proper letter, I can't be bothered to read it," his father had informed him later.

It would have been nice if the late earl had stopped saying things like that since he was dead. But the fact was, Flynn spent most days trying to deal with all of Dunmorey's demands while inside his head he heard the virtually unceasing drone of the dead eighth earl saying, "I knew you couldn't do it."

Save the castle, he meant. Be a good earl, he meant. Be dutiful and responsible and Measure Up, he meant.

If you can.

The implication had always been that Flynn couldn't.

"My lord?" Mrs. Upham persisted.

His jaw tight, Flynn glanced up. He needed to run these figures again, to see if somehow—this time—there was enough to put the new roof on and still get the stables in order by the time Dev brought his new stallion home from Dubai.

There wouldn't be.

He had more chance of hitting the *New York Times* bestseller list with his new book coming out in the States next month. At least he had a talent for hard-hitting interviews, for insightful stories, for the written word.

It was what he'd done—what he'd been good at—before the earldom had changed his life.

But he was not going to give up on Dunmorey, even though the battle to keep the grim old Irish castle from crumbling to bits under his watch was fierce. It was his obligation, not his joy. And frankly, as a younger son, he had never expected to have to do it.

But like everything else in his life these days, he'd inherited while he was making other plans.

His late father would have said it served him right.

And maybe it did.

It wasn't what he would have chosen, but by God, he was determined to show the old man—dead though he was—that he could do it right.

"Everything you need to deal with is here, my lord," Mrs. Upham said. "I'll just throw this nasty old thing out, then, shall I?"

Flynn grunted and started again at the top of the column.

"May I bring you a cup of tea, my lord? Your father always liked a cup of tea with his post."

Flynn ground his teeth. "No, thank you, Mrs. Upham. I'm fine on my own."

He had learned rather quickly that while in Mrs. Upham's eyes, he would never be his father—and thank God for that, Flynn thought—he did have his own version of the Voice of Authority.

Whenever he used it, Mrs. Upham got the point.

"Very good, my lord." She nodded and backed out of the room. He might as well have been the king of England.

He did the figures again. But they still didn't give him the total he wanted. He sighed and slumped back in his chair, rubbed his eyes and flexed his shoulders. He had an appointment with a contractor at the stables in an hour to see what else needed to be done before Dev brought the stallion home in a fortnight.

As the horse was a proven winner and thus a money-making proposition, the stables were an absolute priority. Stud fees and book royalties didn't seem like enough to keep Dunmorey afloat.

The castle had been in the family for more than three hundred years. It had seen better times, and, hard though it was to believe, it had seen worse times as well. To Flynn it was the physical embodiment of the family motto: *Eireoidh Linn*, which he knew from his Irish schooldays meant, roughly, We Will Succeed Despite Adversity.

His father had always told English-speaking guests it meant, We Will Survive!

So far they had; though since the castle was no longer entailed, it could be sold.

They hadn't had to sell it yet. And Flynn was damned if he was going to be the one to lose the fight.

But the post brought more renovation estimates that were depressingly large, and bills that were equally so. They'd borrowed against the castle to get the money to get the stud up and running. When it was, things would be better. If his book did well, they would certainly improve. In the meantime...

Flynn shoved back his chair and got up to prowl the room, cracking his knuckles. It was on his return to the desk that his eyes were drawn to the spot of blue paper in the bottom of the bin.

It was every bit as dirty and crumpled and unappetizing as Mrs. Upham had said. And yet it intrigued him.

It wasn't another bill or another set of estimates. It wasn't a circular about a farm auction or an invitation to Lord and Lady So-and-So's house party. It wasn't stuffy. It wasn't embossed.

And it was, he could see, addressed half a dozen times over, to him. A call from his old life.

"Junk," his father would have said, dismissing it.

But he had never been his father, as they all well knew.

Flynn reached down and fished it out. The original address had been sent to him in care of *Incite* magazine in New York City.

His brows lifted at that. Once upon a time he'd done entertainment personality pieces and feature articles for them. But he hadn't written articles for *Incite* in years. Not since he'd covered what had been dubbed "The Great Montana Cowboy Auction" in tiny Elmer, Montana, six years before.

His father had always called those articles "fluff" and said it was a pity Flynn hadn't been good enough to write real news about something that mattered.

In fact, he had been. And the succession of addresses crossed out on the envelope were pretty much a record of where he had proved exactly that: Africa, the East Indies, west central Asia, South America, the Middle East.

One hot spot after another, each one hotter than the last.

Now he stared at the envelope, caught up in a flickering cascade of memories—of excitement, of challenge, of life.

He studied again the firm but neat feminine handwriting beneath the others. He didn't recognize it. He was amazed that the letter had caught up with him at all. It must have been a labor of love or sheer stubborn perseverance on the part of the world's post' offices. The single U.S. domestic postage stamp had first been canceled in November five years before.

Five years?

Five years ago last November Flynn had been in the middle of a South American jungle, writing a "real news story" on twenty-first-century intertribal warfare—by experiencing it firsthand.

"You sure you want to do this?" His editor in London had been skeptical when Flynn had announced he was going. "You've already been shot once this year. This time you could get yourself killed."

That had been the general idea at the time.

His older brother, Will—"the heir," his father had always called him—had died just months before. And depending how you looked at it—certainly if you looked at it the way the earl did—Will's death had been Flynn's fault.

"He was going to the airport to meet you!" the earl had railed, feeling only his own pain, never even acknowledging Flynn's.

"You're the one who had to come home to recover! You're the one who got shot!"

But not the one who'd died.

That had been Will—steady, sensible, responsible Will who had stopped on the way to the airport to help a motorist change a flat tire and got hit by a passing car.

In a matter of an instant, the world changed—Will was gone and Flynn had become "the heir" in his place.

It was hard to say who was more dismayed—Flynn or his father.

Certainly when he'd recovered from his gunshot wound received pursuing one of those "real news stories that mattered"—the one he'd come home to recuperate from when Will had been killed—no one, least of all his father, had objected when he'd left for the intertribal warfare in South America.

No one had objected when he'd pursued increasingly danger-ous assignments after that.

But no matter how dangerous they were, no matter that he got shot again, more than once, Flynn hadn't died. He'd still been the heir when his father had dropped over from a heart attack last July.

Now he was the earl. He wasn't traveling the world anymore. He was stuck at Dunmorey Castle.

And a five-year-old letter that had chased him around the world and finally tracked him down seemed far less demanding—and much more appealing—than thinking about any of that.

Flynn slit it open. Inside was a single sheet of plain white paper. He took it out and unfolded it. The letter was brief.

Flynn. This is the third letter I've written you. Don't worry, I won't be writing any more. I don't expect anything from you. I want nothing. I just thought you had a right to know.

The baby was born this morning just after eight. He was

seven pounds eleven ounces. Strong and healthy. I'm naming him after my father. Of course I'm keeping him. Sara.

Flynn stared at the words, tried to understand them, put them in a context where they would make sense.

Expect...nothing...right to know...baby.

Sara.

The paper trembled in his fingers. His heart kicked over in his chest. He started again—this time with the signature: Sara.

An image of intense brown eyes, flawless ivory skin and short-cropped dark hair flickered through his mind. A vision of smooth golden skin and the taste of lips that spoke of cinnamon and spice teased his thoughts.

Sara McMaster.

Dazzling delightful Sara from Montana.

Good God.

He stared at the letter as its meaning became clear.

Sara had been pregnant. Sara had had a baby.

A boy...

His son.

It was Valentine's Day.

Sara knew this because last night she had helped her five-year-old son, Liam, print his name laboriously on twenty-one Valentine cards complete with cartoon-art mutant creatures saying, "Be Mine" and "I'm 4 U."

She knew it because together they had covered a shoe box with white paper and red hearts to be his own "mailbox" at kindergarten and because she had baked cupcakes—chocolate ones with chocolate frosting and red and white candy hearts on them—as right before he went to bed Liam remembered he had volunteered to bring the cupcakes for the class party today.

And she knew because—for the first time since Liam was born—she actually had a date.

Adam Benally had asked her to dinner. He was the foreman out at Lyle Dunlop's place. He had come to the valley a few months ago from Arizona. A widower with a past he didn't often talk about, he was at least candid about "trying to outrun his demons." He'd brought the ranch accounting work in for Sara, and that was how they'd got to know each other.

No stranger to demons herself, Sara thought she and Adam might have a lot in common. He at least was getting past his demons. It was about time she got past hers.

"You can't be a recluse forever," her mother, Polly, had told her more than once. "Just because you had one bad experience…"

Sara let her mother talk because that's what Polly did. A lot. And her mother was probably right about the recluse part. It was the "bad experience" part that was the sticking point.

It hadn't been bad. At least not while it was going on. While it was going on it had been the most amazing three days of her life. And then…

Nothing.

That was the bad part. That was the part that made her gut clench every time she thought about it. The part that spooked her, that made her hesitant to ever open up to another man, to ever try again.

But finally she'd said yes. She'd made up her mind to try again with Adam. A dinner date. A first step.

"About time," Polly had said when Sara told her the plan. "I'm glad. You need to banish some ghosts."

No. Just one.

One Sara saw in miniature—right down to the tousled black hair and jade-green eyes—every time she looked at her son.

She shoved the thought away ruthlessly. Now was not the time to be thinking about that. About *him*.

Liam might be a reminder, but *his father* was past. Ordinarily she went whole days without thinking of him at all. It was just today—because it was Valentine's Day, because she'd accepted Adam's invitation, determined to kill two memories with one night out—that he kept plaguing her thoughts.

"Don't," she told herself out loud. The past was over. She'd rehashed it often to kill it from over scrutiny. It had done no good. Now she needed to concentrate on the future—on Adam.

What would Adam expect? She paced the kitchen, made tea, thought about what to wear, how to be charming and make conversation. Dating was like speaking a foreign language she had no practice in. It was something she'd done very little of before—

No! Damn it. There she went again!

Determinedly she carried her mug of tea to the table and laid out files so she could work. If she could get the hardware store accounts finished before Liam got home from school, then she could take a break, maybe go out and build a snowman with him, have a snowball fight. Do something to distract herself.

Liam was going to spend the night at her aunt Celie's who lived up the street with her husband, Jace, and their kids.

"Why all night?" she'd demanded when Celie had offered. "We're only going to dinner. I'm not spending the night with him!"

"Well, you might want to invite him in after," Celie said innocently. "For a cup of coffee," she added with a smile. It wasn't what she meant.

Sara knew it as well as she knew that she wasn't up for anything beyond dinner. Not now. Not yet.

How on earth could she have let six years go by without a single date?

Well, really, she rationalized, when had she had time?

She'd spent the first three years after Liam's birth finishing a degree in accounting, then setting up in business. Between her son and her schooling and the jobs she'd taken to make ends meet, she'd had no time to meet eligible men.

Not that she'd wanted to.

Once burned, twice shy and all that. And while she supposed there was wisdom in the notion of getting right back on a horse once you'd been thrown, there was also wisdom in being a damn sight more cautious the second time around.

She'd been too reckless the first time. This time she was taking it slow and easy and that meant dinner, perhaps a quick peck on the lips. Yes, she could do that.

But first she had to get to work.

One of the pluses of her job as an independent certified public accountant was that she could set her own hours and work from home. That made it easier to be home when Liam was. The downside, of course, was that it was easy to get distracted—like today. There was no boss to crack the whip, to make demands. It was more tempting to think about checking her closet to see what she wanted to wear or to put in a load of laundry, make a cup of tea and talk to Sid the cat when she really needed to focus on work.

So she started again, made herself settle down at the kitchen table, which was also her desk, and spread out the accounts from the hardware store. Adding columns of figures required that she pay close attention and didn't allow her mind to wander, to anticipate, to worry.

A sudden loud knock on the front door made her jump. She slopped tea all over her ledger sheet. "Damn!"

She went to the sink and grabbed the dishrag, mopping up the spill, cursing the delivery man, who was the only one who ever came to the front door. He left her office supplies when she ordered them. But she didn't remember—

Bang, bang, bang!

Not the delivery man, then. He only knocked once, then,

having awakened the dead, he always jumped back into his delivery truck and drove away. He never knocked twice.

Bang! Bang! Bang!

Let alone a third time.

"Hold your horses," she shouted. "I'm coming!"

She stalked to the door and jerked it open—to the ghost of Valentine's past.

Oh, God.

She was hallucinating. Panicking at the notion of dating again, she'd conjured him up out of the recesses of her mind.

And damn her mind for making him larger than life and more appealing than ever. Tall, rangy and narrow-hipped, but with shoulders even broader than she remembered. And just for reality's sake, her brain had even dusted his midnight hair with snowflakes. They should have softened his appearance, made him seem gentler. They didn't. He looked as pantherish and deadly as ever.

"Sara." His beautiful mouth tipped in a devastatingly appealing lopsided grin.

Sara knew that grin. Remembered it all too well. Had kissed the lips that wore it. Had tasted his laughter, his words, his groans, his passion.

Her face burned. Her whole body seemed suddenly consumed by a heat she'd tried to forget. She glanced at her hands knotting together, astonished that they didn't have steam coming off them, the memory of him was so powerful.

"Speechless, *a stór*?" His rough baritone with the light Irish inflection made the tiny hairs at the back of her neck prickle. It felt as if a ghost had run a finger down the length of her spine.

"Go away," she said fiercely, closing her eyes, resisting the hallucination, the memories—the man. It was agreeing to go out with Adam that had done this to her. It had tripped a trigger of memories she'd bottled up, stored away, refused to take out and look at ever again.

She screwed up her eyes and shut them tight. Counted to ten. Opened them.

And felt her stomach plummet to her toes at the sight of him still standing there.

He wore jeans, a black sweater and a dark-green down jacket. He hadn't shaved in a day or two. His cheeks and jaw were stubbled. His eyes were bloodshot. But his impossibly long lashes blinked away snowflakes as he watched her with amusement. And when he grinned a little more at her befuddlement, she saw that he had chipped a tooth. She didn't think she would have hallucinated the chipped tooth.

So he was real. He was everything she remembered.

And worse.

Six years ago Sara had dreamed of this moment. Had held on to the hope that he would come back to Elmer, to her. For nine months she had planned and hoped and prayed. And he'd never come. Had never called. Had never written.

And now—out of the blue—he was here.

Sara's heart turned over, and at the same time, she felt the walls slam down. A fury of pain so fierce engulfed her that she had to swallow and swallow again before she could find her voice.

And when at last she did, she prayed it sounded as flat and disinterested as she wanted to be as she acknowledged him. "Flynn."

Flynn Murray. The man who had taken her love, given her a child and left her without a backwards glance.

It had been her fault. She knew that. He'd never promised to stay. Had never promised anything—except that he would hurt her.

And by God, he'd done that.

At the time, of course, she hadn't believed he could. She'd been nineteen, naive, foolish and in love beyond anything she'd ever dreamed possible. She'd met Flynn unexpectedly when he'd come to their small town to cover the human-interest angle of a celebrity cowboy auction. It had been strange, serendipitous, and almost like finding the other half of herself.

She'd always been practical, sensible, driven. She'd had goals since she was old enough to spell the word. Meeting and falling in love with Flynn had turned them upside down. He'd come to her tiny town and changed her world.

Flynn had made her want things she'd never dreamed of wanting—and for a few days or weeks she'd believed she could have them.

She knew better now.

She knew about hurt and pain and getting past them. She knew she wasn't letting it happen again. Ever.

"You look beautiful," he told her. "Even more beautiful than I remember."

Sara's jaw tightened. "You look older," she said flatly.

And harder. The lines and angles of his face were sharper, his features almost gaunt. He was still handsome, of course. Perhaps even more handsome, in a rough-edged harsher way. At twenty-six Flynn Murray had been all smooth easy smiles, pantherish grace and spontaneous Irish charm. At thirty-two he looked rugged and ragged and battle weary, like a man come home from war.

There were surprising flecks of gray at his temples. And a scar creased his temple and disappeared into salt-and-pepper hair.

Had some jealous boyfriend attacked him when Flynn had charmed a local girl?

Sara wouldn't have been surprised. Living a fast-lane life must be tougher than she'd ever imagined. How hard it must be, Sara thought mockingly, tracking celebrities all over the globe.

Flynn's mouth tipped ruefully and he shrugged. "You know what they say—it's not the years, it's the miles."

"And you've gone quite a few, I'm sure," Sara said acidly. And he could keep right on going. She didn't need him here now. Didn't need him upsetting her life, her hopes, her son.

Oh, God, Liam. A shaft of panic shot through her. He couldn't have ignored Liam for five years just to turn up now, could he?

"What are you doing here?" she demanded.

And as if he could read her mind as well as disrupt her life in every other way imaginable, Flynn said, "I want to meet my son."

CHAPTER TWO

SARA'S jaw set. She steeled herself against his words, his intent and, mostly, against the green magic of his eyes.

"You're a little late," she said through her teeth. *About five and a half years.*

"I am." He nodded gravely. "I just found out."

Just found out? She blinked her disbelief. "Yeah, right." There wasn't enough sarcasm in the universe to flavor her response.

But Flynn didn't seem to notice. He was rummaging inside his jacket, pulling a small manila business envelope out of an inner pocket. He opened the envelope and extracted a dirty creased faded blue one. Wordlessly he held it out to her.

Sara stared at it. Then, slowly, she reached out and took it from him with nerveless fingers.

The paper looked as if it had been trampled by a herd of buffalo. She turned it over and saw at least half a dozen addresses printed and scrawled and scratched out, one on top of another. One word caught her eye: *Ireland.*

That was a surprise. Six years ago he'd been delighted to be out of the land of his birth.

"Nothing for me there," he'd said firmly.

Like her ancestors 150 years ago, she'd supposed. Her dad had often told handed-down stories about their own family's desperate need to leave and find a better future for themselves. Though Flynn had never said it, she had no trouble believing it had been true of him, too.

Now, curious about his change of heart, she glanced from the envelope to the man. But his green eyes bored into hers so intently that her own skated away at once back to the envelope.

It had originally been a pretty robin's-egg blue, part of a set with her initials on it that her grandmother had given her at high school graduation. Sara hadn't had the occasion to write many letters. She still had some sheets of it left.

But this letter she remembered very well.

She had written it only hours after Liam was born. She had known that there was little chance Liam's father would heed it. He hadn't paid any attention to her previous two letters, not the first one telling him she was pregnant, not the later one telling him again in case he hadn't got the first one.

He'd never replied.

She'd understood—he wasn't interested.

But still she'd felt the need to write one last time after Liam's birth. She'd given him one last chance—had dared to hope that news of a son might bring him around. She wasn't proud. Or she hadn't been then.

Now she was. And she was equally determined. He wasn't going to hurt her again.

"I didn't know, Sara," he repeated. He met her gaze squarely.

"I wrote you," she insisted. "Before this—" she rattled the envelope in her hand "—I wrote. Twice."

"I didn't get them. I was...moving around. A lot. I wasn't writing for *Incite* anymore. They sent it on. So did others. It kept following, apparently. But I didn't get it. Not until last week. Then I got it—and here I am."

Sara opened her mouth, then closed it again. After all, what was there to say? He'd come because he'd discovered his son. It still had nothing to do with her.

It shouldn't hurt after all this time. She'd known, hadn't she, that she didn't matter to him the way he'd mattered to her. But hearing the words still had the power to cut deep.

But she was damned if she was going to show him her pain. She crossed her arms over her chest. "So? Should I applaud? Do you want a medal?"

He looked startled, as if he hadn't expected belligerence. Had he thought she'd fall into his lap with gratitude, for heaven's sake?

"I don't want anything," he said gruffly, "except the chance to get to know my son. And do whatever you need."

"Go away?" Sara suggested because that was definitely what she needed.

Flynn's scowl deepened. "What? Why?"

"Because we don't need you."

But even as she said it, she knew it was only half-true. *She* didn't need him. But Liam thought he did.

"Where's my dad?" he'd been asking her for the past year.

If he wasn't dead, why didn't he come visit? Even divorced dads came to visit, he told her with the knowledge of a worldly kindergartner. Darcy Morrow's dad came to see her every other weekend.

"He can't," Sara said. "If he could, he would." It wasn't precisely a lie. Even though she'd believed Flynn had deliberately turned his back on them, she knew telling Liam that would be absolutely wrong. It wouldn't be wrong to say his father would come if he could. He simply couldn't—for whatever unknown reason. End of story.

Fortunately, Liam hadn't asked why. But when told at school that Thanksgiving was a family holiday, he'd wondered again why his dad wasn't there. And then he'd said, "Maybe he'll come at Christmas!"

"Don't get your hopes up," Sara had cautioned. But telling Liam that was like telling the sun not to rise.

"I'll take care of it," he'd said, and when they went to the mall in Bozeman, mortified Sara by marching right up to Santa, telling him that for Christmas he wanted his father to come home.

Sara had been prepared for tears on Christmas morning when no father appeared. But Liam had been philosophical.

"I didn't get my horse at Grandma and Grandpa's right away, either," he'd said. "I had to wait till spring."

Because, of course, the colt hadn't been born till spring. And now? Sara could just imagine what Liam would say when he came home this afternoon.

"He should have a father," Flynn said now. "A father who loves him."

There was something in his voice that made Sara look up. But he didn't say anything else.

"He's fine," she insisted. His life might not be perfect, but whose was? "You don't need to do this."

"I do," he said flatly.

"He's not here."

"I'll wait." He looked at her expectantly. She didn't move.

He cocked his head and studied her with a look on his face that she remembered all too well. A gentle, teasing, laughing look. "You're not afraid of me...are you, Sara?"

"Of course I'm not afraid of you," she snapped. "I'm just... surprised. I assumed you didn't care."

The smile vanished. The look he gave her was deadly serious. "I care. I mean it, Sara. I would have been here from the first if I'd known."

She didn't know whether to believe him or not. She did know

she wasn't going to be able to shut the door on him. Not yet. She was going to have to let him in, let him wait for Liam, meet his son.

And then?

He was hardly going to be much of a father if he was in Ireland. But at least Liam would know he had one who cared.

But first she would need to set some ground rules. So, reluctantly, she stepped back and held the door open. "I suppose you might as well come in."

"And here was I, thinking you'd never ask." He flashed a grin, the one that said he knew he'd get his way.

Sara steeled herself against it—and against the blatant Irish charm. She stepped back to let him pass—and to make sure not even his sleeve brushed hers as he came in.

But as he passed through the doorway, he stopped and turned towards her. And he was so close that she stared right at the pulse beat in his throat, so close that it wasn't his sleeve, but the chest of his jacket that brushed against the tips of her breasts, so close that when she drew in a sharp breath, she caught a whiff of that heady scent of woods and sea that she remembered as purely and essentially Flynn. Her back was against the wall.

"Did you miss me, Sara?" he murmured.

And Sara shook her head fiercely. "Not a bit."

"No?" His mouth quirked as if he heard the truth inside her lie. "Well, I've missed you," he said roughly. "I didn't realize how much until right now."

And then quite deliberately he bent his head and set his lips to hers.

Flynn Murray had always known how to kiss. He had kissed her senseless time and time again. She'd tried to forget—or at the very least tried to assure herself that it was only her youthful inexperience with kissing that had made her body melt and her knees buckle.

She'd told herself it would never happen again.

She'd lied. And this kiss was every bit as bad—and as marvelous—as she had feared.

It was a hungry kiss, a kiss determined to prove how much he'd missed her. And it was—damn it all—mightily persuasive. It tasted, it teased, it possessed.

It promised. It promised moments of heaven, as Sara well knew. But she wasn't totally inexperienced now. She knew it also promised years in the aching loneliness of hell.

She lifted her hands to press against his chest, to push him away, and found her hands trapped there, clutching at his jacket, hanging on for dear life as every memory she'd tried so hard to forget came crashing back, sweeping her along, making her need, making her ache, making her want.

Exactly as she had needed and ached and wanted before. Only, then she'd believed he felt the same.

Now she didn't. Couldn't. Not and preserve her sanity. Not if she didn't want to be destroyed again.

Flynn had come, yes. But he'd come because of his son—not because of her.

And despite his kiss—the sweetness, the passion, the promise—and because of his kiss—its ability to undermine her reason, her common sense, her need for self-preservation—she had to remember that.

She'd loved him six years ago, and he had left her.

He'd made no promises, but she'd trusted. She'd given him her heart and her soul and her body. He had known her on a level no one else ever had. She'd believed he loved her, too. She'd believed he'd come back.

He never had.

Not until today. Not until he'd found out about Liam.

He wanted his son. Not her.

Finally she managed to flatten her hands against his chest and give a hard, furious shove.

He stumbled backwards awkwardly and, to her amazement, fell against the nearest chair. "Damn it!"

But it wasn't her he directed the words at. He muttered them to himself as he staggered, then winced and shifted his weight onto his left leg. Sara didn't know which stunned her more—the kiss or the fact that he was clearly favoring one leg and moving with none of his customary pantherlike grace.

Still trembling from the kiss, she asked, "What happened?"

"I got shot." The words were gruff and dismissive.

She felt as if they'd gone straight to her heart. "Shot?" She gaped, then told herself it probably served him right. Maybe he'd played fast and loose, loved and left a woman who got angrier even than she had. "Take advantage of one too many women?" she asked. Given the fast-lane celebrities he wrote about, it seemed all too likely.

"Assassin."

"What?"

"He wasn't trying to kill me." He shrugged. "I was in his way."

Sara swallowed, then shook her head. "I don't understand." She wasn't sure she wanted to, but it was better to be distracted by assassins than kisses. She shut the door and stepped around him into the room.

"I was in Africa." He mentioned a small unstable country she'd barely heard of. It made Sara blink because there certainly weren't any celebrities there. "He was trying for the prime minister. He missed. At least he missed the prime minister. Gave me a little souvenir to remember him by." His mouth twisted in a wry smile.

None of it made sense to Sara.

The Flynn she'd known went to New York and Hollywood and

Cannes, not Africa. And even if he had gone there, prime ministers were hardly the sorts of celebrities he wrote about. He wrote features about starlets and rock stars, actors like her stepdad and, at a stretch, soccer stars and tennis pros.

But she didn't have a chance to ask anything else.

She hadn't heard the back door open, hadn't heard the footsteps pound across the kitchen floor, hadn't heard anything until the door into the living room and dining room flew open.

And Liam burst into the room.

CHAPTER THREE

DEAR God, the boy was Will all over again.

And the sight of him would have sent Flynn reeling if kissing Sara hadn't already done so.

She'd given him a shove, of course, and, with his bad leg, that had been enough to send him off balance literally. But emotionally just the sight of her had already rocked him. And the kiss, well...Flynn had kissed his share of women over the years, but none of them had been like kissing Sara.

He wanted to think about his reaction—and hers—analyze it, understand the effect she had on him. But there was no time. Not now.

Now he stood stunned and staring at this vital bouncing ball of energy, this miniature version of his dead brother.

Intellectually Flynn had known that his son would likely resemble his Murray forebears. But actually seeing it was astonishing.

The boy—Lewis, if she'd named him after her father—was the spitting image of his brother. The same black unruly hair, same fair skin, same spattering of freckles, same thin face and pointed chin. Same build, too. Wiry. Slender. There was a coltish boniness even beneath the boy's winter jacket and jeans.

The boy didn't spare him a glance. He came hurtling into the room, with no regard for the stranger in the living room. His eyes—as green as Will's and Flynn's own—went straight to his mother.

"Look!" He wriggled off his backpack at the same time he was thrusting a white box covered with hearts into his mother's hands. "I musta got a skillion Valentines! An' I got a real fancy one from Katie Setsma. She must like me!" He flung his backpack onto a chair, then scrambled up on it to pull off his boots.

Sara shot Flynn a quick glance, as if she were trying to gauge his reaction to this astonishing little person. The words in a crumpled letter and the living breathing bouncing reality were two entirely different things. He wondered if he looked as dazed as he felt.

"Of course she likes you, Liam," she said to her son.

And that nearly did Flynn in.

"Liam?" he said hoarsely. The Irish shortened form of *William*? Flynn's hand groping blindly for the back of a chair to steady himself.

At his voice, the boy stopped jerking off his boots and, for the first time, looked at Flynn curiously.

Instantly wary, Sara stepped between them. "That's what we call him," she said firmly. "I told you I named him after my father, Lewis William. But he's not my father. He's his own person." She said this last fiercely as if defying him to argue.

He didn't. Couldn't. Could barely find his voice—or words. "I…yeah. I'm just…surprised." He sucked in a hard breath and tried again. "It was my brother's name—William. Will. We called him Will."

Sara caught the operative tense. "Called? Was?"

"He died." Flynn ran his tongue over suddenly parched lips. "Almost six years ago."

Their gazes met, locked. Sara looked shocked then, too. And there were a thousand unasked questions in hers. He couldn't answer them. Not now at least.

"I'm sorry," she said quietly. And there was the sound of real regret in her voice. "I didn't know."

It made Flynn's throat tighten. He gave a jerky nod. "I know that. It's just—" he gave his head a little shake "—one more surprise."

And then the room went silent. No one moved. No one spoke. Finally he grew aware of the sound of Liam sliding off the chair and coming around by Sara. He stopped and looked up at his mother, as if trying to figure out what was going on, as if hoping she would tell him. But she didn't speak, didn't even seem to see him, and her gaze never left Flynn.

The boy's gaze followed hers. Will's eyes—Dear God, they really were—fastened on him, then narrowed a little in the same way Will's always did when he assessed something or someone new.

There was no doubt the boy had picked up on the current of apprehension that pervaded the room. He was like a fox scenting danger, Flynn thought.

And then, apparently deciding what was necessary, he deliberately moved in front of Sara, his back to his mother's legs as if he would protect her. His chin jutted out as he contemplated Flynn. There was no sparkle now. Just the hard unwavering green gaze that generations of Murrays wore when protecting their own.

"Who're you?"

It was the question Flynn had been anticipating since he'd made up his mind to come to Montana. It was the question he'd been longing to answer.

And suddenly he found the words stuck in his throat. After a hundred—hell, after a *thousand* at least—visualizations of the moment when he would meet his son, he didn't have the spit to say a word.

He opened his mouth and nothing came out. For the first time in his entire life, Flynn Murray had no words.

Sara, too, was staring at him expectantly, waiting for him to say something. He couldn't. He shook his head.

Maybe she realized he couldn't—or maybe she simply decided that taking charge herself was a better idea. Her hands came down to rest on the boy's shoulders and squeezed lightly. When she spoke, her voice was soft.

"He's your father, Liam."

Liam's eyes flew wide open. So did his mouth. He stared at Flynn, then abruptly his head whipped around so he could look up at his mother. His whole body seemed quiver with the unspoken question: *Is that true?*

Sara's smile was faint and a little wary. But she gave the boy's shoulders another squeeze, then nodded.

"He is. Truly," she assured him. "He's come to meet you."

For a long moment Liam still searched her face. But then, eventually, he seemed satisfied with what he saw there. He turned back to Flynn. His gaze was steady and level and curious as he stared at his father in silence. The silence seemed to go on—and on.

And then, finally, in a slightly croaky but determined voice, Liam asked, "Where've you been?"

Absolutely mundane. Absolutely reasonable.

Absolutely devastating.

Flynn swallowed. "I've…I've been a lot—" he cleared the raggedness out of his throat, glad he at least had a voice now. He started again "—a lot of places. All over the world. I'd have been here sooner. But…I didn't know about you."

Liam's gaze jerked around to challenge his mother's. "You said you wrote to him."

"She did," Flynn answered for her. This wasn't Sara's fault. "Your mother wrote me before you were born. She wrote me later when you were born…but I didn't get the letter. Not for a long time. Years." He picked the envelope up from the top of the bookcase where Sara had set it and held it out. "Take a look. It's been everywhere. But I didn't get it until last week."

Liam's gaze shifted from Flynn's face to the letter in his outstretched hand. But he stayed where he was, so Flynn moved closer.

Still the boy didn't reach out right away. But finally he plucked the envelope from Flynn's fingers and turned it over in his hands, then studied the multiplicity of addresses on it.

"I was working a lot of different places all over the world," Flynn explained awkwardly. "It must have missed me everywhere I went. It finally caught up with me back home. In Ireland."

Liam didn't look up. He was rubbing his thumb lightly over the words on the envelope, staring at the writing, which, Flynn realized suddenly, he wouldn't be able to read yet. He wasn't old enough. "All those addresses are places I was," he explained.

Then Liam looked up at him. "You live in a castle?"

Flynn blinked. He *could* read?

Apparently so, for Liam was pointing at the one address on the envelope that hadn't been scratched out. "That's what it says." He scowled at it, then sounded out, "Dun-more-ee castle." Liam read it out slowly then looked up again. "That's your house?"

"No, dear," Sara began, but Flynn cut in.

"It is. Dunmorey Castle."

He heard Sara's sharp intake of breath. Liam's eyes went so wide that his eyebrows disappeared into the fringe of black hair that fell across his forehead. "You live in a *real* castle? With a moat?"

"I live there. And it is a real castle in name," Flynn qualified, looking at Sara for the first time, seeing accusation in her gaze. "Mostly it's a huge drafty old house," he went on. "Over five hundred years old. Mouldering. Damp. And it does have a turret and some pretty high walls. But it doesn't have a moat."

"Well, that's something, I guess," Sara muttered.

"No moat?" Liam's face fell. His brows drew down. "What makes it a castle then?"

"It was a stronghold. A really old fort," Flynn explained. "Where people could go if they needed to defend themselves against invaders. And it was where the lord of the lands lived. The boss," he added in case that made more sense. "That's what makes it a castle."

Liam digested that. "Can I see it?"

"Of course you can."

"A picture, he means," Sara said hastily. "Can he see a picture? Of your *castle*." Her tone twisted the word as if she were blaming him for it.

The damn place was no end of trouble. Flynn shook his head. "Not with me," he told Liam. "But I can get you some. Even better, I can take you there. You can see it in person."

Liam gaped. "I can?"

"No!" Sara said sharply.

Liam twisted around to look up at her. "I can't?"

"It's in *Ireland*," she explained, shooting Flynn a furious glance. "That's clear across the ocean. Thousands of miles."

"I could fly on a plane." Liam was undaunted. "Couldn't I?" He glanced around at Flynn for confirmation.

"You could," Flynn agreed. "Best way to get there, in fact. We'll talk about it." He smiled at Sara.

Sara's mouth pressed into a tight line. "I don't think we'll be talking about it anytime soon." She turned to her son and said firmly, "He can tell you all about his castle, Liam. But do not expect to go zipping across the ocean."

"But I've never seen a real castle."

"You're five. You have plenty of time," Sara said unsympathetically. "And in the meantime you can make them out of Legos."

Liam brightened. "I already did." He spun towards Flynn. "It's sort of real. But it doesn't have a moat either. Wanna see it?" He was all eagerness now, hopping from one foot to the other now, looking up at Flynn.

The expression on his face now didn't remind Flynn so much of Will as it did of the young Sara—when he had first met her. She'd had that same sparkle, that same eager, avid, intense enthusiasm.

Right now she was glaring at him, her jaw locked.

He had made a living out of reading people, picking up their body language, understanding when to move in, when to back off. He had no trouble reading Sara. She wasn't thrilled to see him and, he supposed, he didn't blame her. He hadn't been here when she needed him.

But he'd come when he found out, hadn't he? They'd get it sorted. They had to. But they weren't going to do it now in front of their five-year-old son. So he gave Sara a quick smile that, he hoped, appeased her for the moment, then turned to Liam. "I'd like that."

"C'mon, then!" And Liam was off, pounding up the stairs.

Flynn looked at Sara. She glared. Then she shrugged. "Oh, hell, go with him. But don't you dare encourage him to think about jetting off to Ireland!"

"It's possible, Sar'. Not immediately but we should discuss—"

"No, we shouldn't! Damn it, Flynn, you can't just pop up and disrupt our lives. It's been *six* years!"

"I didn't know—"

"And you didn't *want* to know," Sara said, "or you'd have come back."

"I thought—"

"I don't care what you thought. You knew where I was. I didn't leave! If I'd mattered at all, you'd have come back. You never came!"

"You were going to med school."

She stared at him. "Do I look like I went to med school?"

He blinked, then shook his head, dazed. "What do you mean? How should you look?"

"I got pregnant, Flynn. I had two and half years of university left for my bachelor's. I had a baby. It was all I could do to get through that. I didn't go to med school."

"But—"

"Circumstances change. Plans change."

"Yes, but—" He couldn't believe it. She'd been so driven. "Is that why you're so ticked at me?"

She stared. "What? Because I couldn't go to med school? Of course not! I don't care about that. I got my degree. I have my own business. I'm a CPA—certified public accountant. I like my work. I like numbers in boxes. I like adding things up and having them come out right. I like knowing the answers! Speaking of which, what the hell is this about you living in a castle?"

He shrugged, still trying to come to grips with Sara as a CPA, not a doctor as he'd always imagined. Sara as a mother had been tricky enough. But Sara changing her determined plans boggled his mind. She'd been so committed, so determined. She'd said flat-out that nothing was going to stop her.

"Castle?" she prompted, when he didn't answer immediately.

"I inherited it," he said dismissively.

"You told me there was nothing for you in Ireland!"

"There wasn't. I wasn't supposed to inherit, I didn't want to. My brother died." He got angry all over again just thinking about it. Sometimes he wanted to strangle Will—except he wanted his brother alive. That was the whole problem.

"Will," she said, making the connection.

"Will." It always felt like a lead ball hitting him in the stomach when he said his brother's name.

Sara pressed her lips together. "Well, I really am sorry about that. It was…a shock, I gather."

"An accident. Coming to get me at the airport."

A mixture of pain and sympathy flickered across her face. "Oh, God."

"Exactly."

Their gazes met again. The connection that had been so strong seemed to be flickering back to life—and Flynn couldn't believe how astonishingly happy that made him feel.

And then, as if she shut the light off, Sara's expression went blank. "You'd better go see the castle," she said, pointing through the door to the kitchen. "Just through there and up the stairs."

Thank goodness he went after Liam.

Sara didn't know how much longer she could have stood there and talked rationally—well, almost rationally. Her heart was hammering. Her hands were trembling. She had to get a grip. Had to stop flying off the handle at him. Had to stop caring!

For years she'd managed to convince herself that she didn't—that her three days of aberrant behavior with Flynn Murray had been some sort of alchemical reaction that would never be repeated.

And all it had taken was the sight of him standing on her doorstep and she was in meltdown all over again.

It was the shock, that was all. He was the last person she'd expected to see when she'd opened the door this afternoon. And the sizzling awareness she'd felt when she'd seen him had caught her off guard.

She didn't even want to think about what had happened when he'd kissed her!

But thinking about him with Liam wasn't much better.

They were so much alike.

Sara had always known that Liam resembled his father. But without pictures—and try as she had to find any of him among all those taken during that hectic February weekend, she'd discovered none—she'd told herself Liam simply had his father's coloring. After all, she occasionally saw glimpses of herself, her own father, her mom, even her brother Jack in her son.

But when Liam and his father were in the same room, she didn't only see glimpses of Flynn in her son. He was almost a clone.

But even more than Liam's features, it was his body language that was so much like his father's. He moved like Flynn, with the same intensity of purpose. And when he was stymied, he even prowled around rooms like Flynn.

Both Flynn and Liam were edgy, intense, determined. When Liam wanted something—like building a castle or learning to read—he went after it. Like his father. And while Liam was still occasionally little-boy clumsy, Flynn, even with his limp—dear God, she still couldn't believe he'd been shot!—was clearly powerful, controlled and in command. Sara was sure that Liam would be exactly like that one day, too.

She wondered if Flynn saw it.

She wondered exactly what Flynn did see—and what he was really doing here. To see his son, yes. She could accept that. But what else did he want? What *more?*

He wasn't going to waltz in here and try to take her son away from her, was he?

Just because he lived a in castle now, he didn't need to think he could take over her son.

Or was it just her son he had in mind?

The memory of that kiss snuck back in to torment her—the memory of his lips on hers, the possessive hunger of that kiss! Surely he didn't want her again?

Of course he didn't. If he had, as she'd told him, he'd have come back long before this. God knew he could have had her then.

But this had been a power play, pure and simple. He was just proving he could still make her react, could still—let's face it, Sara, she said to herself—turn her on.

And yes, damn it, he could. He had! He'd nearly swept away her reason, had made her weak with longing, with wanting him exactly the way she'd wanted him all those years ago.

But at least this time she'd managed—barely—to resist. And she would not let it happen again. It could only happen, she assured herself, if he caught her unawares.

But there would be no more "unawares." Now she was fore-warned. Flynn Murray had burned her once. There was no way she was letting him do it again!

Thank God she was going out with Adam tonight.

All of a sudden her lukewarm attitude towards their Valentine's Day date had undergone a definite change. Focusing on Adam would be far better than spending the evening at home thinking about Flynn.

She glanced at her watch. It was quarter to four. She didn't know how long he expected to stay, and she didn't want to follow them to Liam's bedroom and ask. Even from the kitchen she could hear Liam's excited chatter and Flynn's low baritone re-sponses. She could hear that blasted Irish lilt in his voice. God, it was seductive. Even now—forewarned, forearmed—it had the power to raise goose bumps along her spine and make the back of her neck tingle.

"Adam," she said aloud. "Think about Adam." She had to get ready to go out with Adam.

Resolutely she climbed the stairs. At the end of the hall she could see into Liam's room, could see Liam darting past the doorway, talking a mile a minute, could see Flynn's long legs stretched out as he sat on Liam's bed.

She did not want to think about Flynn in the same sentence with the word *bed*.

She got her clean clothes from her own room, then headed for the bathroom, calling out as she went, "I'll be in the shower."

It was only to let them know where she was. She hoped to heaven Flynn didn't think it was an invitation!

Of course he didn't. But it didn't stop her face from flaming. She was mortified to see how red it looked when she glanced in the bathroom mirror. "Stop it," she commanded herself. "Stop thinking about him."

Of course, that was easier said than done. She showered quickly—and used mostly cold water, not wanting to think why it seemed suddenly such a good idea. She washed her hair and blew it dry. Then she dressed in the black velvet pants and red cashmere sweater that her sister Lizzie had given her for Christmas.

She had worn a red sweater the night she had gone to Flynn's motel room. And the memory almost had her pulling the sweater back over her head and looking for something else. But to do so would give him more power over her than he deserved.

He deserved no power at all.

Besides, she thought with all the dispassion she could muster, he probably wouldn't even have the vaguest notion of what she'd worn. He hadn't cared about her the way she had about him.

Flicking a brush through her hair, then putting on some lipstick that she dared hope she would not gnaw off, she gave herself one last stern look, then opened the bathroom door.

It was completely quiet. There was no sound of Liam's eager chatter now, no Irish lilt from Flynn. The light in Liam's room was off.

Had Flynn had enough already and left?

It was a happy thought—followed immediately by, *Then where was Liam?*

She hurried downstairs. No one was in the kitchen, either.

"Liam?"

She got no answer. He'd better not be playing hide-and-seek without telling her. When he was four he'd thought it fun to dart into the closet and stay still as a mouse while she went nuts looking for him. But he was five now—nearly five and a half— and she'd told him off in no uncertain terms. He knew better. He'd moved on to other sins—like sneaking in TV cartoons when he thought she wouldn't notice.

"You'd better not be watching television, young man," she said, marching across the kitchen and sticking her head around the door to look in the living room, expecting to find him in the semidarkened room with the sound turned down.

But only Sid the cat was there, sleeping on the couch. He raised his head and gave her a baleful look before closing his eyes again.

Sara was not given to panic. She had learned not to. But now her heart began to pound. She spun back into the kitchen.

"Liam!" Her voice rose.

Where *was* he? He wasn't supposed to go anywhere without telling her. Another of his sins. He'd been in trouble for going to Celie's during Christmas vacation without telling her he was leaving. She'd come down on him like a ton of bricks. He wouldn't do it again.

Would he?

Now she saw that his jacket was gone. His boots were gone.

And so was Flynn.

No!

He wouldn't! He'd never—

I'll take you to Ireland, he'd said. And she'd refused to discuss it.

He couldn't have just walked in and taken off with her child!

She ran to the back door and jerked it open. "Liam!" She was desperate now, frantic as she ran out onto the snow-covered porch. *"Liam!"*

"What?" The small surprised voice came from around the side of the house. It sounded quite close and completely bewildered.

Oh, God. The surge of relief nearly melted Sara's bones. Her legs wobbled and she gripped the pillar at the top of the stairs as, a second later, Liam's head poked around the corner.

"You don't have to yell. I'm right here," he said indignantly.

"So I…see." She was still gasping for air. Her heart was still slamming against the wall of her chest. "Where's Flynn? Where's your…father," she amended, still breathing hard.

"Right here." Liam jerked his head towards the side yard. "We're buildin' a castle." He gave Sara a thumb's-up and grinned broadly. "Like Dunmorey."

Sara was still gulping air, still bashing down the panic, when Flynn came around the corner of the house. It had begun to snow again and his midnight hair was dusted with sparkling white snowflakes. He looked rugged and handsome and gorgeously reminiscent of the first time she had seen him.

She started trembling.

His intent green gaze fixed on her. "Something wrong?"

"No. I just—" she dragged in a breath "—didn't realize you'd gone outside." Her fingers still gripped the porch pillar. "I thought…"

But she couldn't admit what she'd thought, couldn't acknowledge aloud her terror at the belief—even for a split second—that he'd done the most devastating thing of all: taken her son.

She shook her head. "I didn't know where he was. I thought… never mind. Just…carry on." And with those words she turned abruptly and hurried back into the house, shaken, relieved and shattered all at the same time.

She shut the door and sank down into one of the wooden kitchen chairs, trying with trembling fingers to peel of her snow-soaked socks.

The back door opened, and Flynn strode in.

"You thought I'd taken him." His words were flat. His eyes accused her.

She tried to quiet the shaking and forced herself to concentrate on peeling off the socks before she would answer. Then she stood up, needing to be on a level with him, needing to find her self-control before she could reply. "I didn't know what you'd done."

But she couldn't deny her panic—it was still there in her voice and she was sure he could read it on her face.

Flynn's jaw tightened. He pushed the door shut behind him.

Sara shot a glance towards the side yard. "Liam—"

"He's building the turret. I told him I wanted to see it when he was done. And I will see it," he said firmly, "but not before we get this straightened out."

Sara swallowed and straightened, not liking his tone. "Get what straightened out?" Her voice was steadier now. She wished her nerves were.

"What you obviously think. I did not come to steal my son away from you."

She bristled at the words "my son." But she knew he was just making a point. "I didn't imagine—"

"You damned well did!"

"All right, fine. I did. But only because he was gone! And you'd said you'd take him to Ireland! What was I supposed to think? I'd finished showering and dressing and you weren't there!"

"What sort of man do you think I am?" His eyes were stormy now, a turbulent sea green.

He didn't wait for her to answer that. She wasn't sure she could have, anyway. She didn't actually know what sort of man he was, did she? Once she'd thought she had, but that had been all wrong.

"We talked about Dunmorey," Flynn said patiently, as if explaining things to a small, not-too-bright child. "And we talked about forts and building castles and it was snowing and we decided it would be fun to build a snow castle. Okay? We didn't go to Ireland. We were in the garden."

Sara nodded numbly, knowing she should feel foolish, still feeling the residual effects of her momentary panic. "You didn't say," she mumbled.

"I didn't realize you wanted me to stick my head in the bathroom and announce it." A corner of his mouth quirked, and the way his eyes slid over her made her wish she had a suit of armor on, not a cashmere sweater and velvet pants.

She wrapped her arms across her chest. "Of course not!"

He didn't reply for a moment, as if considering what to say. Then he shook his head gravely. "I'm sorry you were upset. It never occurred to me to tell you. I thought you'd figure it out."

"Well, I didn't. I didn't know what you'd do. I don't even know you."

"You did," he said quietly, and the serious husky tone of his voice sent those goose bumps skittering down her spine again.

She hugged herself. "No."

But he nodded. "You did, Sara." His tone was insistent. "I think you knew me better than anyone else on earth."

"Then why—" The anguished words burst from her before she could stop them. But fortunately she managed to shut her mouth before she sounded like a pathetic twit. And thankfully, the phone chose that moment to ring.

She spun away from him and grabbed for the phone on the countertop. "Hello?"

"Oh, dear. You already know." It was Celie, sounding worried and apologetic.

"Know?" Sara echoed. She braced a hand against the counter. Celie wasn't going to tell her about Flynn, was she? The Elmer grapevine being what it was, that was distinctly possible.

"About Annie." Annie was Celie's four-year-old. "I thought you must from the tone of your voice. You sound…weird. Upset. Because I can't babysit tonight. She's running a fever. They sent her home from preschool. She's vomiting now. You don't want Liam here tonight."

"No, I—"

"I'm so so sorry."

"It's all right," Sara said. "I'll work something out."

"Maybe Jace could come down when he gets back from Billings, but it won't be until late and—"

"No, really, it's fine. Don't worry. I…have to go. Hope Annie's better soon." She hung up and stayed facing the cupboard for a moment, getting her equilibrium back before she turned around. It would be all right, she assured herself. She just wouldn't go.

"Trouble?" Flynn asked when she finally turned around.

Sara shrugged. "Celie was going to babysit Liam tonight. Now she can't."

"Where were you going?" There was something so proprietary in Flynn's tone that it set her back up.

"On a date."

His brows drew down. "With who?"

"Obviously, you wouldn't know him. His name is Adam. He's the foreman at one of the ranches nearby. And he's a sculptor, too," she added. It was true and it was definitely impressive. She'd seen some of Adam's work.

Flynn's jaw tightened. "Is it serious?"

"His sculpture?"

His eyes narrowed. "No, damn it. You and him. Adam." He fairly spat the name.

Sara blinked. "What difference does it make?"

"I want to know how things stand."

He wasn't the only one, Sara thought. Only, what she wanted to know about had nothing to do with Adam. "We're dating," she said ambiguously. "And it is Valentine's Day," she added, because why not let him think it was more serious than it actually was?

Besides, Adam was a chivalrous sort of guy. He probably wouldn't mind her hiding behind her date with him. All of a sudden going seemed far smarter than staying home.

"Excuse me now," she said, reaching for her little local phone list. "I need to find a babysitter." She picked up the phone and began to punch in the number.

Flynn took the phone out of her hand. "I'll watch him."

"Don't be ridiculous."

"What's ridiculous about it? He's my son."

"No."

"Why not?"

"He doesn't know you."

"He wants to. He told me he asked Santa for me." Flynn grinned.

Sara wanted to spit. "He's five. And curious."

"So, fine. Let him get to know me. Let me spend time with him. What better way?"

It sounded like the way to perdition to Sara. She shook her head. "It's too soon."

Flynn scowled. "Oh? And when is it not going to be too soon, Sar'? Tomorrow? Next week? Next year?"

"You've been here two hours, if that!"

"And I would have been here sooner if I'd known," he said evenly. "I'll say it again—as many times as it takes—I didn't know. And if you're worried about whether he'll stay with me, ask him."

"What?"

"Ask him if he minds. If he doesn't want me to do it, I won't." Flynn raised his brows, met her gaze, threw down the gauntlet again. "Ask him."

As if on cue, Liam yelled from outside, "Dad! C'mon! What're you doin' in there? Aren'tcha comin'?"

Sara winced at the eager tone, winced at the memory of her son striding up to Santa and saying, "I want you to bring my dad home."

Flynn's gaze remained fixed on her. His expression said all it needed to. But then he added, "Does Adam make you hot when he kisses you, Sara?"

"Fine," Sara snapped. "Babysit. I wish you the joy of it!"

CHAPTER FOUR

FLYNN wished for the joy of it, too.

Babysitting his son while his son's mother went out with another man was not what he had planned.

He'd planned—at some point after Sara had opened the door and bowled him over—to charm her and tease her as he once had done. And then, when he'd soothed her ruffled feathers, he'd intended to take her and Liam to dinner.

He had never considered how high Sara's defenses would be—and how much work he might have to do to make her remember how good it had been between them.

God knew, he remembered. And he was remembering more every minute.

He hadn't let himself think about her—about their time together—for years. What point would there have been?

They had met coincidentally, had clicked instantly. But in truth they had been ships passing in the night—Sara resolutely on her way to medical school and then to save the world, and he determined to shake the dirt of Ireland and Dunmorey off his boots and then to prove to his old man that he wasn't the useless fool the old man seemed to believe.

Just because he wasn't the solid, dutiful lord-of-the-manor type that Will was, didn't mean he didn't have his own talents, his own gifts. Not, Flynn thought wearily, that he had ever managed to convince the old man.

He had an uphill fight convincing Sara that he meant to do right by her and Liam, too. He didn't suppose that grabbing this Adam jerk by the throat and throttling him would go very far in making that point. Sara had never been especially impressed by the caveman approach, as he recalled.

So, fine. He could wait. He could even let her go out with another man—especially one whose kisses didn't make her go up in flames. And this guy's clearly didn't. She wouldn't have been so furious at his question if they had.

But he wasn't going to sit by and let the guy think he had a clear field. No way. So when he heard the knock at the back door and heard Sara open it, he stood up from where he'd been sitting on the sofa looking at old photo albums with Liam.

A few moments later she came into the living room by herself. The Date was apparently on his own in the kitchen.

"He doesn't even come to the front door for you?" he asked Sara as she grabbed her coat from the front closet.

"No reason. He's used to coming in the back door," she said, turning and swishing away towards the kitchen.

Used to? How often did he come in, for God's sake? Flynn's jaw tightened. "Here," he said. "Let me help you with that." He reached for her coat.

"It's all right," she began, still moving. But he twitched it out of her hands and shook it lightly, then held it out for her to slip her arms into.

She tossed him a quelling look over her shoulder, but then stuck one arm into one sleeve and the other into the other. He stepped forward and settled the coat on her slim shoulders, came close enough to breathe in the scent of her shampoo, to catch a whiff of that mixture of spice and sunshine that he'd never smelled anywhere or on anyone but Sara.

It was an intoxicating blend of wholesomeness and seduction. He wondered if she had any idea how enticing she smelled. He bent his head forward to let his nose brush against her hair, to dare to touch his lips to the back of her neck.

She jumped and jerked her head around to look at him, to glare at him.

He smiled guilelessly. "What?"

Her cheeks were almost as red as her sweater. "Nothing," she muttered, rubbing at the back of her neck. "I just—never mind." She stepped away quickly and began to talk rapidly. "I left my cell phone number on the pad on the kitchen table," she said in a businesslike fashion. "You can call Celie if you need anything immediately."

Like to be murdered, Flynn imagined. If Sara wasn't glad to see him, he had no illusions about how her family must feel. "Thank you," he said politely. Then, before she could leave him behind in the living room, he said, "I'd like to meet this guy."

"Why?"

"Color me curious," he said lightly.

"Well—" She hesitated.

"Ashamed of him?"

She shot him a furious look. "Fine. Come and meet him." Then she turned to Liam "No television," she told him firmly. "It's a school night. Get into the bath by eight. I put clean pjs on your bed. I want you in them and in bed at eight-thirty."

"I know," Liam grumbled. Then he looked up calculatingly, "What if Dad says I can stay up later."

"He won't," Sara said, fixing Flynn with a hard stare. "8:30," she repeated to Liam. She bent to give him a kiss, then straightened and looked at Flynn again. "And I mean it."

"Of course." He smiled and she looked at him suspiciously.

"I don't have to go," she said fiercely. "If you think for one minute you're going to undermine—"

Flynn raised his hands and shook his head. "Relax, Sar'. It'll be fine. We'll be fine. Won't we, bud?"

Liam nodded vigorously. There was another knock on the door.

Sara looked as if she would have liked to stay and argue the point further, but finally she just shook her head and turned to go through the door into the kitchen.

"Back in a sec," Flynn promised Liam, and followed Sara.

"I'm all ready," she said briskly to the man standing by the door. And Flynn knew she would have opened the door and disappeared into the night without looking back unless he said something.

"Sara."

She turned back, looking annoyed. "What?"

"Aren't you going to introduce us?" Flynn asked silkily.

One more hard look, but then she shrugged. "Of course." She opened the door wider and put her hand on the sleeve of a very handsome man, who had straight black hair and dark piercing eyes.

"Adam," Sara said in a soft smiling voice that set Flynn's teeth on edge. "You'll never guess who turned up today. This is Liam's father." And then she turned to Flynn. "This is Adam Benally."

So Adam had a name but *he* was simply "Liam's father"?

I don't think so, Flynn thought grimly and, doing his best to minimize his damned limp, strode across the room to claim the kitchen as his territory, offering a hand to Sara's surprised suitor. "Come in," he invited. "I'm Flynn Murray."

The other man's hooded eyes widened fractionally and his gaze flicked toward Sara for a moment before coming back to settle on Flynn. His grip was lighter than Flynn's own, but his hand was hard and callused.

"About time," he said mildly.

The reproach made Flynn stiffen. But if this Adam thought Flynn was going to back down, he was out of luck.

"It is," Flynn said smoothly. "But I'm here now." So back off, he felt like saying. He remembered a story about one of his less-than-civilized ancestors locking his beautiful bride away in the turret to keep her from being ogled by the countryfolk. All of a sudden he felt a certain sympathy with the blighter. And he knew for a fact that he'd never felt this possessive about Dunmorey.

"Can you believe he just got the letter I wrote him five years ago telling him about Liam?" Sara broke in quickly.

Adam looked skeptical. "You don't say."

Flynn didn't. He just stood his ground, met Adam's gaze wordlessly and proprietarily until Adam said, "We have reservations for seven. We need to get going." He looked expectantly at Flynn.

"That's the other thing," Sara went on. "Annie's sick, so Celie can't babysit tonight. Flynn has offered to stay with Liam."

"Flynn?"

"Got a problem with it?" Flynn demanded. "Liam's my son."

Adam looked at Sara. "Are you sure you want—"

"She's sure," Flynn cut in. It was the tone of voice that made Mrs. Upham jump and say, "Yes, my lord," every time he used it.

Adam didn't jump, but Sara did, maneuvering them both out the door. "If we need to be there by seven, we'd better go. You have my number," she told Flynn. "But I'm sure you won't need it."

It was less a comment than a command.

Flynn ignored it. He followed them to the door and stood glowering at them as they went down the steps and along the path towards Adam's fancy pickup truck. "Sara?"

She turned.

He smiled. "I'll be waiting up for you."

* * *

It was Valentine's Day—a time for soft music, warm hearts, tender glances, romance with a capital *R*.

And Sara spent it with Adam—thinking about Flynn.

It made her crazy. *He* made her crazy. He—Flynn. Not he—Adam.

Adam was charming and easy to be with, a man of many talents and definite sex appeal. And tonight he exerted himself to be a good dinner companion, a witty conversationalist, a terrific date.

But it was Flynn whose smile she remembered, Flynn whose words echoed in her brain.

"I'll be waiting up for you," he'd said, that lilt, that charm, that innuendo in his tone!

Well, of course he would be, she rationalized, because he had to be. He was babysitting their son.

But was that what he'd meant? Or was he implying something else? Was he hinting that something would happen when she got home?

Her mind flicked back instinctively to their kiss that afternoon. She shoved it away, tried to focus on Adam. Managed it for all of thirty seconds. But then a thought of Flynn would intrude again. And a memory of the kiss. Flynn, kiss, Flynn, kiss, Flynn, kiss. It happened over—and over—again.

It was not the most spectacularly successful evening.

And when Adam yawned and said he had to be up early to feed cattle, Sara was ready to leave.

The snow had stopped. The night was clear and sharp and cold as they walked back to the truck. They walked so close together that their shoulders brushed. If it had been Flynn, no doubt sparks would have flown. Adam opened the door for her and she climbed in.

They rode back to Elmer in silence. And Sara knew she'd been a disaster of a date. "I'm sorry," she began as he pulled around the corner behind her house.

Adam shrugged. "Now we know."

Did they? Sara supposed they must. She felt guiltier than ever and wondered if she should offer to pay for her half of dinner.

The porch light was on. Was Flynn standing in the kitchen looking out from between the crack in the curtains?

No, that wouldn't be his style, Sara decided. If she didn't immediately come inside, he'd probably open the door and come out and stand on the porch. Jerk!

She climbed out of the truck without waiting for Adam to come around and open the door for her. He raised a brow. She shrugged.

"Because we know," she explained.

"Are you and he—?"

"We're Liam's parents. That's all," Sara said firmly.

"I don't think he's convinced," Adam told her.

"Well, he's going to have to be." She turned to face him. "Thank you for tonight."

"Do you need me to come in?"

She shook her head. "It will be fine." Certainly better than if they reenacted the gunfight in the *OK* kitchen which seemed to be the direction in which Flynn had been headed earlier.

Adam looked doubtful. "You're sure?"

"I'm sure." And then she lifted up to brush a kiss on Adam's cheek. As a thank-you, nothing more.

"Take care of yourself," he said gruffly.

Sara nodded. Heaven knew she was going to try.

She expected to see Flynn in the kitchen, sprawled in one of the chairs, smirking at her, checking his watch and chuckling at how early she'd returned from her date.

But only the cat was waiting. He looked hopefully at his food dish and meowed, but the packet of food she'd set out for him had vanished, so she knew Liam had done his job.

"You're fine," she told Sid who meowed a denial, but who purred when she bent to scratch his ears. "Where is everyone?"

Well, she knew where Liam was. Had Flynn fallen asleep on the couch?

She pushed open the door to the living room so she could hang her coat in the closet and have an excuse to see if Flynn was there. But it was empty, too. The family photo albums he and Liam had been looking at earlier were gone from the coffee table, though. He must have taken them up to look at them with Liam.

Sara hung up her coat, then climbed the stairs. Everything upstairs was dark and silent. Only the night-light in the hall and the one in the bathroom were on.

Had he fallen asleep with Liam, then?

She peeked into Liam's room. Her son lay, as always, on his back with one arm outflung, the comforter wadded up over his middle, the quilt half on the floor. He was the only one there. Carefully, she covered Liam up again and bent to kiss his forehead and his silky hair.

Then, frowning, Sara went back out into the hall. Surely he hadn't left. Even Mr. Here-Today-Gone-Tomorrow Flynn Murray wouldn't be that irresponsible!

"Flynn?" She called his name softly.

She heard a sound. Muffled. Faint. From down the hall.

"Flynn?" She moved back towards the stairway, then heard it again.

And suddenly realized where it was coming from!

How dare he! Sara stalked down the hall to the only other bedroom—hers!—and shoved open the door.

Flynn Murray was sprawled, fast asleep in her bed.

CHAPTER FIVE

SARA stopped dead in the doorway. Her breath caught in her throat.

She was furious—and curious—at the exact same time.

She wanted to stalk straight in there and shake him, wake him and send him on his way. And she knew damned well that shaking him awake would be the worst possible thing she could do.

Confronting a tousled gorgeous Flynn Murray who was already in her bed was a disaster waiting to happen. She needed to turn around and walk away right now.

Every sane sensible cell in her body screamed at her to do exactly that.

But when had she ever been sane and sensible where Flynn Murray was concerned?

Sara clutched the edge of the door frame to keep herself anchored right where she was. But it didn't help. The mere sight of him drew her.

And it wasn't as if she expected anything from him, she thought. She had already used up a lifetime's worth of dreams on this man. She was under no illusions now. She could look with impunity.

Well, maybe not with total impunity, but she knew better than to hope—or dream.

In fact it might be salutary to look at him. It could bolster her immunity to him, help to steel her against any aberrant, tempting thoughts that threatened to undermine her resolve.

And so, carefully, she peeled her fingers away from the door frame and edge closer. Just to look. To see more clearly what the previous six years had done to him.

It was easier—safer—to look at him when he had his eyes closed and was sound asleep.

And so she did. She looked. Then she moved closer still. She stood by the bed and drank in the sight of him. Couldn't help it. She'd dreamed of him so long.

He lay sprawled on his stomach, one arm flung out, his tousled hair midnight dark against the white of the sheet. The shadow of stubble on his jaw was less obvious now, but she remembered the soft scratch of it against her skin six years ago. And the tips of her fingers itched to reach out and brush across it, to feel its roughness now.

Sara clenched her fists, as if she needed to keep them under control, make them behave. *She* needed to behave.

But she couldn't stop staring at him.

For all that she had Liam to remember him by, she had so few other real memories. They'd had three days together—and one amazing night. And since much of that night had been spent in lovemaking, she'd had little opportunity to simply feast her gaze on the man she loved.

Had loved, she corrected herself sharply. *Had.* Past. Very past. No longer.

She didn't love him now. Didn't. Did N.O.T.

She tried to think about Adam, to say his name over and over in her head—but it was no use. He was a lovely man, but not for her. They would doubtless have discovered that anyway. Flynn's presence tonight had merely made it clear much sooner.

She glared at him now—hating him for spoiling all other

men. Hating him for being able to simply walk back into her life after six long years and turn her world upside down.

Hating him for being sound asleep, dead to the world, completely unaware—and making her want him even now.

As if aware of her thoughts, he sighed and shifted—took up even more of the bed. His muscular body was flung across her bed with the same abandon as his son's. His features were a grown-up version of his son's. But the similarities ended there.

Liam was wriggly and cuddly. His father was strong and powerful, even in sleep. His bare shoulders were broad, his arms were well muscled. How a man could get those kind of muscles writing articles absolutely amazed her. He moved restlessly, and the quilt slipped lower.

Was he naked in her bed?

Sara sucked in a sharp breath. Her palms felt suddenly damp and her heart skipped a beat. Quickly she backed up a step. But she didn't flee.

Still she watched. Wondered.

Playing with fire, she cautioned herself. At any moment he could wake, open his eyes and find her staring down at him. He could rise and shed the quilt that covered him and draw her down into his arms.

She wouldn't go! She wouldn't. She hoped.

Still she swallowed carefully, as if the noise of the muscles in her suddenly dry throat would wake him.

She tried to think logically. A part of her wanted to shake him awake, to say, "I'm home. You can leave now." A part of her wanted to crawl in beside him.

She wasn't going to do either.

She had heard him tell Liam he'd flown from Dublin to Seattle, then to Bozeman, and then had driven to Elmer. She couldn't imagine how many hours he'd been awake. It was no wonder he'd crashed.

But in her bed!

Did he expect she would just blithely slide in with him?

Probably he did. After all she supposed he'd simply think that they had shared a bed before. So it would be no big deal. Besides he had to have realized that afternoon that she still wasn't indifferent to his kiss.

Which was exactly the reason she wasn't about to do it.

But she couldn't make him drive back to his motel room in Livingston, either—not after he'd babysat—not to mention smacking a bit too much of obvious self-preservation.

So she crept around the bed, snagged her flannel nightgown off the hook inside her closet door, careful not to step on the floorboards that creaked. Unfortunately, the closet door squeaked despite her best efforts.

At the sound Flynn muttered and rolled onto his side. Sara held her breath, then, when he didn't move again, she grabbed her robe, too, and tiptoed out of the room.

In the bathroom, she stripped off her clothes and pulled on her nightgown. She was shivering and would have loved a hot bath, but the noise of the pipes was legendary.

It would surely wake Flynn. And she had no desire to confront him sleepy and in his underwear—provided he was wearing any. It was far too reminiscent of the night she'd gone to his hotel room. He'd been in a T-shirt and boxers then, not expecting company. He'd looked stunned to see her, had told her it was a bad idea.

And fool that she was, she hadn't believed him.

Now she did. And so she made sure she was as quiet as possible. She brushed her teeth, washed her face, then crept back down the hall into Liam's room where the spare bedding was stored in an old chest. From it she dragged out a patchwork quilt that her great-grandmother had made before her own daughter was born, and then gathering it in her arms, went back downstairs.

Sid met her at the bottom with a curious "Mrrrrow?"

"Shh." She bent and scooped him up on top of the quilt and carried him across the icy kitchen floor, through the dining room and into the living room.

There she dropped him onto the Morris chair, then settled on the sofa and tugged the quilt around her. It didn't win any prizes for comfort.

Sara was only five feet five. The sofa was less. She bent her knees and cursed her stupidity for having declined Sloan and Polly's offer of a new sofa last Christmas.

"Sure you don't want a sleeper sofa?" her mother had asked. "One of us might want to come and stay with you," she'd suggested with a grin.

"Exactly why I'm keeping the one I've got," Sara had retorted, also grinning.

They both knew that Celie's house had more than enough room to put up however many extraneous McMasters and Gallaghers might turn up in Elmer and want a place to stay. Besides, Sara didn't like having things handed to her.

Now, though, she thought she might have made a mistake. The sofa had lumps, too, and—

"What the hell are you doing?"

Sara jerked bolt upright at the sight of Flynn's dark form silhouetted in the doorway. She grabbed the quilt and clutched it like a shield against her chest.

"What does it look like I'm doing? I'm going to sleep."

"Here?"

"Where else? You were in my bed!"

"Noticed, did you?" A slash of white teeth grinned at her. There was a hint of amusement in his voice now, but Sara wasn't laughing. She felt too vulnerable.

"I noticed," she said stiffly. "And I realized you were probably jet-lagged, so I let you sleep. Instead of waking you up and sending you on your way," she added righteously, scooting back farther into the sofa because Flynn was no longer in the doorway. He was coming toward her.

"Very kind, I'm sure. But entirely unnecessary. Come to bed, Sara." His voice was low and husky and sent a shiver of longing down her spine.

"I'm in bed," she said firmly.

"The sofa is too short to sleep on."

"Did you try it?" she challenged.

"Anyone longer than Liam wouldn't fit. Besides—" he loomed over her now "—I wanted to be in your bed."

Sara's heart slammed. She tugged the quilt up higher and folded her arms across it as if that would keep it from leaping right out of her chest.

"No comment?" Flynn queried. "It seemed like a grand idea to me."

"Why?" Sara said gruffly, hating that she sounded breathless.

"Because I was dead tired." He paused. "And because I didn't want that cowboy getting into your bed."

"Oh, for heaven's sake! You thought I would go to bed with Adam? With Liam in the house?" She was outraged at the very notion.

"Obviously not. What about at his place?" The teasing tone was gone now.

She wrapped her arms tighter across her chest. "That is none of your business."

He studied her in the darkness, then shook his head. "You wouldn't," he decided. Then, "You haven't," he added, sounding supremely satisfied.

"How do you know?" Sara demanded indignantly. It was one thing to be particular about who she slept with. It was another to have Flynn act like it was all on account of him. Even if it was.

He smiled down at her. "Because deep down you're still the Sara you were six years ago." She could see the whiteness of his T-shirt and boxers in the moonlit reflections that poured in the windows off the snow. The rest of him was, by contrast, still shadowy and dark. But he was close enough that she could have reached out and touched him. Her fingers clenched around the quilt.

She glared up at him. "And how do you know that?"

He waved a hand at her. "Look at you. You're trying to sleep on a couch the size of a walnut. You're sitting there, uptight as a fireplace poker, that quilt wrapped around you like it was armor. If sex were casual for you, you wouldn't have hesitated getting in bed with me."

"Just because I did once—" she said bitterly.

"You loved me."

"Did," she agreed because there was no denying it. "The more fool I. Besides, I was a child."

He shook his head. "You weren't. You were one hell of a woman, Sara."

In a perverse way his words nourished a part of Sara—the womanly needy part of Sara, the part that had always felt he'd left because she'd failed him—the way rainfall fed a desert land.

But another part—the rational sensible part—heard the same words for the "Here be dragons" warning that she really needed to heed. Whether or not she'd been—or still was—one hell of a woman, she didn't need to get swept away by this man again.

Once was all any sane woman could stand.

"Go away, Flynn," she said wearily. "Go back to bed. Get some sleep. Or drive to Livingston if you're awake enough."

"I'll be staying then," he said easily, "as you've invited me."

"I didn't—"

"'Go back to bed,' you said. 'Get some sleep.' And I will." He held out a hand. "Come with me."

"Not on your life."

"You can't sleep here."

"Yes, I can."

"You'll be miserable. You won't get a wink of sleep lying on this thing." He nudged the sofa with his foot and offered his hand again. "Come on. I won't touch you."

"You couldn't not touch me! The bed's not that big."

"Fine. I'll touch you. But I won't make love to you. Is that what you want? Will you ever get a better offer?" he said mockingly.

It wasn't what she wanted. But what she wanted—Flynn Murray's undying love—she could never have.

"Go away, Flynn," she said past the lump in her throat.

He stood, hovering above her, not going away at all. And she had the panicky feeling that he might just pick her up and carry her up the stairs. But then she thought with the relief of reflection, he couldn't do that. His leg wouldn't let him.

"Damn it, Sara," he muttered, and she got the feeling the thought had crossed his mind, too—and so had the realization that he couldn't just do what he wanted anymore.

Even so, he didn't turn and stalk back upstairs the way she wanted him to, either. In fact, neither of them moved. The grandfather clock ticked loudly, but no louder, Sara thought, than her heart was pounding.

The cat jumped up on the sofa, startling her. "Oh!"

He butted her with his head, then stepped onto her knees, determined to knead them into a sleeping spot. His claws poked her through the quilt and her nightgown. Still she didn't move.

Neither did Flynn.

Then suddenly he turned around and Sara breathed a sigh of relief—until he flung himself down on the sofa next to her!

"Right, then," he said expansively. "We'll just stay here."

She sat up straight and scrunched herself against the arm of the sofa. It was barely more than a love seat. The words took on new meaning. "Flynn, stop it! Don't be an idiot!"

"Eejit," he corrected her. "That's the way we say it in Ireland. At least get the pronunciation right." He slanted her a grin, then stretched out his long bare legs, crossing them at the ankle and spread his arms along the back of the sofa. A male animal staking his territory, a green-eyed panther taking over a den, making himself at home.

In her home! And Sara knew that if she moved back even a fraction of an inch, she would end up leaning against him.

But he didn't touch her.

He'd said he wouldn't—and he wasn't. She wanted to kill him.

The clock ticked. The cat purred. She and Flynn sat in silence. The only other sound was of them both breathing.

Sid kneaded her thighs, then turned and kneaded some more. She gritted her teeth against the sharpest claws in Montana. Or maybe it was just that right now she had the most heightened senses in Montana.

She could feel the heat emanating from Flynn's body. He was that close. So close that she could stick out a finger and run it down over his ribs. She could loosen her grip on the quilt and touch his bare thigh.

She couldn't let herself think like that!

Finally Sid settled down, and the purring grew even louder. It seemed to take over the room.

She and Flynn sat in silence on the sofa. And Sara wondered if they would stay like this forever. Would Liam come down in the morning and find the two of them stiff as boards?

Probably. Because Flynn seemed determined to wait her out

And he had, by far, the more comfortable seating arrangement. He had three quarters of the sofa, too, though he wasn't using it.

A hiss of annoyance passed through Sara's teeth.

Flynn gave a jaw-cracking yawn, then looked her way. "I'm not responsible if I touch you when I fall asleep," he informed her.

"Go upstairs."

"Not without you."

"For heaven's sake! This is ridiculous."

"It is," he agreed solemnly, "as there's a nice comfortable reasonably good-size bed upstairs just waiting for someone with half an ounce of sense to use it."

"Some*one*," Sara said pointedly.

"Some*ones*," Flynn corrected himself. He reached across his body with his left hand and scratched Sid behind the ears. His hand was now right over her lap. But he wasn't touching her. Just the cat.

Sara didn't breathe. Or move.

"Maybe even a cat if he's lucky."

He would let the cat come, too?

She darted a quick glance in his direction. In the moonlight she could see the shadows of his profile, the hard planes and sharp angles of his face. She could also see a shadowy crease of a scar on his jawline that she hadn't noticed before.

"Another gunshot?" she asked before she could stop herself.

Flynn lifted his hand from Sid's head and ran it along the edge of his jaw and nodded. "That it was. You came very close to never seeing me again at all."

He said it lightly enough, but she realized he was serious and that truly terrifying things had happened to him during the six years she'd imagined him covering all sorts of gossipy entertainment news.

"Why did you do it?" she demanded, needing to know. The

questions she hadn't asked seemed to bubble up urgent but unbidden now.

Flynn shrugged. "Because I was young and stupid and thought I was invincible and immortal." His hand stilled for a moment, then he drew a long breath and went back to scratching Sid's ears. But he stared straight ahead, his gaze fixed on something in the unknowable darkness. "And because I needed to prove I could."

"Not to me," Sara said quickly.

She did not want to be responsible for him nearly dying, thank you very much.

"Not to you," he agreed. "Though I will say you were something of an inspiration."

"I never—"

"You were such an idealist. So bloody determined. Life wasn't a lark to you."

But it had been to Flynn. She knew that. It was one of the things that had so appealed to her about him. He had energy and determination, but he didn't take everything as seriously as she did. He'd made her smile. He'd made her laugh. He'd taught her that there was more to life than duty and determination. There was also love.

For all the good it had done her.

"You inspired me," he told her. "But it was my old man was showing."

Sara could understand that. She and her mother had not always had the most genial of relationships. Polly had always been casual and scattered and easygoing. Far too easygoing, Sara had thought for many years.

It was only since she'd got pregnant and become a mother herself that she'd begun to understand that Polly's apparent lack of concern wasn't any such thing. It was a matter of prioritizing and not obsessing about things—and people—who could take care of themselves.

She didn't know what Flynn's issues with his father were.

For all that they had spent three days focusing almost entirely on each other, she realized now that she had been the object of most of their discussing. And while Flynn had told her about his life and his likes and dislikes, he'd never talked about his family besides mentioning an uncle who was a priest in New York. She didn't think he'd talked about his father at all.

"Did your father live in the castle?" She could see why having a father who lived in a castle might make a person feel the need to live up to something.

"He did. It's where I grew up."

"Good heavens." He must think her house was a shack.

His mouth curved. "It's not exactly your typical storybook castle. No moat, as I told Liam. It's more of a Renaissance-age fortress. Of sorts."

She wasn't sure what a Renaissance-age fortress of sorts connoted. But it sounded foreboding. "And you live there now?"

He nodded. "I do. As Murrays have these five hundred years."

She couldn't help staring at him. "You're joking."

He gave a shake of his head. "I'm not."

Sara stared in astonishment. "How come you never mentioned it…last time?" She didn't want to think about "last time" but she couldn't help saying that.

Flynn shrugged. "Because it wasn't my problem then. I was my own man. It had nothing to do with me. But then Will died. He was the heir," he explained. "To the earldom. I was the spare—then."

"Earldom?" Sara echoed. She felt suddenly hot and cold and totally disoriented.

"The earl of Dunmorey," he said wearily and rubbed a hand over his face. "The ninth earl, as a matter of fact. The old man was the eighth. He died last summer."

Sara sat in stunned silence. Nothing—absolutely nothing!—

was the way she'd thought it had been. And then she rounded on him indignantly, not even caring that her knees bumped into his thigh. "You lied to me."

"I did not!"

"You said you'd come to America to seek your fortune!"

"And so I had. I wasn't the heir. I had to make my own way. The old man had his ideas of how I ought to live my life. The priesthood was mentioned. Medicine. Something Worthy." He nearly spat the word. "All fine and good, but not for me. He didn't approve of anything I did. I didn't give a damn. We had row after row. And I walked out. Came over here to find my own way, make my own life."

She had never heard so much emotion from Flynn. She wondered now that she'd thought she'd loved him—or that he'd loved her—when it seemed she hadn't really known him at all.

"And did you find it?" she asked after a moment.

"I thought so. I was spinning my wheels, though, when I came here. You challenged me."

"I?" Sara was incredulous.

He nodded. "Made me want something more valuable. Made me want to use my talents—my writing—but do it right. And I was. I still will. I'm a writer. That's what I do. It's how I earn my living. And that won't change. But—" he sighed "—I have other duties now. Other responsibilities."

"Because you're the earl?"

"Because I'm the earl."

He said the words as if the weight of the world lay upon them—and on him. The quicksilver Flynn of six years ago was gone. She wondered now if he even existed or if he'd just been a figment of her girlish imagination.

They had been so wrapped up in each other those few days—and yet they didn't seem to have really known each other at all.

The only thing Sara knew now was that his attitude towards the castle, the earldom—his duties and responsibilities—echoed the way he'd sounded this afternoon when he'd announced he was here to see his son.

"Liam's not a castle," she said, her voice adamant.

Flynn had been staring straight ahead, but at her words his head snapped around and he stared at her. "What?"

"I mean it. He is not a responsibility you need to shoulder. An obligation. A duty to be taken care of. He's a child. A little boy. A real live person!"

"I know that, damn it!" His tone was clipped. Angry almost.

Sara tried to search his face, to see what she could read in his expression. But there wasn't enough light to see clearly. He was the one sitting rigidly now, and she shifted, shrugging her shoulders, inadvertently touching his arm where it lay along the back of her sofa. She stayed where she was, turned to face him. "I just…need to be sure."

"Rest assured. I know all about not being a person," he said grimly. "You don't need to ever remind me about that."

She wanted him to explain. Was he talking about his relationship to his father?

There was so much about him she didn't know. And was afraid to ask for fear she would want to know more. And more. Because for all that she realized now that she hadn't really known him well at all six years ago—despite what he'd said—she knew her feelings for him made her vulnerable.

And that hadn't changed. If she weren't careful, she would find herself right back in the same place she'd been six years ago—in love with a man who didn't really love her, who was only interested in their son.

She pressed her lips together and turned away to stare out the window. It was all shadows of silver and gray, nothing clear. Nothing definable. Like her life. Mere hours ago she'd known exactly where she was going and what she was doing. And now she knew….

She didn't know what she knew.

The silence grew…and grew.

Then Flynn said, "I don't see Liam as just a responsibility. He is, of course. Mine as well as yours, but I want more than that."

Sara stiffened.

"I want to be a real father to him. The kind of father mine never was."

"You live in Ireland!" Sara pointed out. "You're an earl."

"Not my fault," Flynn said roughly, "though my father might disagree. And being an earl does not automatically disqualify me from being a good father."

"You are not taking him to Ireland!"

"I told you I am not taking him away from you. We can all go—"

"No!"

He didn't say anything then. Just sat there in silence. Watched her in the darkness. Made her wary. Made her suddenly weepy. Made her want—want things she'd hoped she was over wanting. Why had he come back?

And if he had had to come back, why now? Why not five years ago when she could have believed he loved her? Or why not five years from now when she might have met another man and fallen in love with him, married him, had his children?

Why *now?*

"Don't worry about it, Sara," he said quietly. And there was a tenderness to his voice that made her ache even more.

"I'm not worried," she said gruffly against the lump in her throat. "I'm fine."

"Of course you are." Still gentle, as if he was trying to soothe a skittish horse.

Sara would have bristled, but she was suddenly too tired. She felt drained, exhausted. Her muscles hurt from sitting up straight so long, and she allowed herself to sag back just a bit. Her back touched his arm. But as he made no move to wrap it around her, she just stayed where she was.

"Go to bed," she muttered.

"When you do," he said with a smile. He didn't move.

She shot him an irritated look.

He shrugged. "Up to you."

"Then I'm staying here," she said stubbornly.

"As am I," Flynn replied and flexed his shoulders, then settled in more comfortably.

"I mean it," Sara said.

"As do I."

But before it could become any more ridiculous, there was a sudden sound from beyond the kitchen. "Mama! Mom?"

Liam's panicky shout from the top of the stairs brought her straight to her feet. She dropped Sid to the floor as she stumbled over the quilt.

"It's all right, Liam. I'm downstairs," she called, already running up them.

He was standing at the top, clutching the Curious George monkey that Jack had given him when he was two. He wasn't crying, but he gulped before he spoke.

"Where were you?" His breathing was rapid, his voice broke.

"I told you. Downstairs." She wrapped her arms around him. "It's all right. Did you have a bad dream?"

He shook his head. "Nuh-uh. I woke up an' I went to look out an' see the castle we built—in case I dreamed it. But I didn't. It's there." He hiccupped.

"Yes, I know." She cuddled him close.

"An' my dad." Another hiccup. "I thought I'd dreamed my dad."

"No, Liam. You didn't dream him."

"I…I know. On account of the castle an' the king." He bobbed his head. "Didja see the king?"

"King?"

"I was gonna show you, but when I went to your room, you weren't there."

"I know. But I'm here now."

He sniffled and rubbed his nose on his pajama sleeve. "Good. C'mon. I'll show you the king. You can see him from my room." And, trauma receding, Liam took her hand and led her down the hallway into his room. He pushed open two slats in the blinds. "See?"

Sara knelt beside him and looked down at the castle that he and Flynn had built in the afternoon. In front of it she saw now that they'd built a snowman, as well.

"A king. See?" Liam pointed. "He's got a crown an' a…an' a…" he groped for the word.

"Sceptre," Flynn said from behind them.

Liam spun around, a grin splitting his face. "You're here!" He gave a little wriggle of happiness.

"I am here," Flynn said firmly.

Liam's joy and the obvious bond they'd begun to build were both evident.

"Time to go back to sleep," Sara said firmly and drew Liam to his bed and tucked him in firmly. "If you don't you'll be all groggy and begging to stay in bed when it's time to get up for school."

Liam shook his head adamantly. "Nope. I gotta go to school. I gotta tell 'em my dad's here."

"Fine, you do that," Sara said. She bent and gave him a kiss, then straightened and brushed a hand over his hair.

"Dad, too," Liam insisted. And he held up his arms for a hug.

And Flynn, understanding the body language, bent awkwardly into their embrace, his injured leg off-balancing him. But he ignored it, hugging the boy hard and giving him a kiss, too.

Sara, watching, felt something very like a pain deep in her chest. Because it was so wrong? Or because it was so right? She wished she knew.

"Go to sleep now," Flynn said gruffly.

"You'll be here in the morning?" Liam demanded

"I'll be here," Flynn promised.

"I thought you were goin' to Livingston."

"I stayed."

Liam looked at his father for a long moment, then his head swiveled so his gaze met Sara's. She didn't have to see the light shining in his eyes to know it was there.

"Don't—" she began.

"Don't worry about a thing, Liam." Flynn cut in. "Just go to sleep now." And he reached over and would have grasped Sara's arm as if to draw her out of the room.

But Sara was having none of that. She stepped away and bent over Liam to give him a kiss. "Do not get any ideas," she told him firmly.

"But—"

"None." She tapped him on the nose with her fingertip, then straightened and marched out of the room, leaving Flynn to follow her.

He did. But before she could go past her own room and head back down the stairs, he caught up with her, took her arm and drew her in, then shut the door firmly behind them.

"What do you think you're doing?"

"You want him to go to sleep?" Flynn leaned against the door so she couldn't get past him. "Then get in your own bed. If you go back downstairs he's going to wonder what's going on."

Sara opened her mouth to argue, but knew it was true. If she went back downstairs now, Liam would be out of his bed in a flash, coming after her, sensing that all was not as it should be.

He would expect her to go into her own room to sleep.

But not with Flynn!

Although that probably wasn't even true, Sara realized grimly.

In Liam's world, mothers and fathers shared beds. Grandma and Grandpa did. Aunt Celie and Uncle Jace did.

So why wouldn't she and Flynn?

She sighed, trapped.

"It'll be all right. I'll even go downstairs if you want," Flynn told her. "Once he's gone to sleep."

Sara hesitated, shivering, though whether from the cold or something else she couldn't have said.

Flynn noticed. "Come on, Sar', you're freezing." And he pushed away from the door and somehow herded her backwards until the backs of her knees bumped against the mattress and abruptly she sat down on the bed.

He sat beside her and took her cold trembling fingers in his hands and chafed them between his. "Get under the covers."

"I don't—" she began.

But he didn't let her finish her sentence. He picked up her legs and shifted her into the bed beneath the covers, then settled himself alongside her, spooned his body against her back and wrapped an arm around her waist to draw her hard against him.

"There," he muttered. His mouth was so close that the word stirred the hair against the back of her neck.

"You said you wouldn't touch," Sara grumbled.

"And you said I wouldn't be able to help it. You were right." He snuggled closer, tucked his arm more tightly around her. "Now shut up and go to sleep."

"I can't."

"Then shut up and let me go to sleep." And she felt him burrow closer, settle in.

"Flynn—"

"Shh." He sighed. Snuggled. His breathing slowed.

Sara lay there, tense and trembling. Mostly disbelieving. She was in bed with Flynn Murray?

To sleep? Oh, sure. She held herself rigid and unmoving.

"Sara." His lips tickled her ear. "Relax."

As if. But she couldn't hold herself as stiff as a barge pole forever. Unconsciously her muscles began to ease. Flynn moved again experimentally, settling against her.

"Better," he sighed. His breathing slowed. His arm that curved over her waist relaxed, his fingers opened. Yet all the while his body pressed hard and warm and enticing against hers.

Any second now Sara knew he would make his move. He would nibble her ear. His hand would curve possessively over her belly or would move up to brush against her breasts. He would touch. He would tease. He would torment.

And she would resist, Sara was determined. She would resist!

And then Flynn emitted a soft faint noise. And then another. He was asleep.

He hadn't slept so well in years.

Flynn sighed and stretched and shifted, coming around slowly, savoring the feel of it, of the soft sheets and comfortable mattress, the cold air and warm quilt. He didn't know where he was, only that he felt better than he had in...well, "forever" didn't seem too much of a stretch of things.

He wasn't at Dunmorey.

He knew that without even opening his eyes.

There, his first conscious awareness was always of the sound of rain dripping in the pails in the hallways or of the icy dampness of the room that he couldn't afford to heat or of the oppressive weight of responsibility for it that he wasn't meeting. He didn't feel that now.

He wasn't in any of the thousand-and-one hotels, rooming houses and dirt bunkers he'd lived in while in pursuit of a story, either. There the sense of edgy urgency always made him shoot out of bed almost before his eyes were open.

He felt settled. At home. Centered.

And as if someone was watching him.

His eyes flicked open.

Green eyes peered into his.

"Will?" he croaked, and instantly realized his mistake, felt the pain of loss and the joy of realizing who this really was all in an instant. "Hey, Liam."

His son.

Liam broke into a broad grin. "I knew it! I knew you'd be awake. I told Mom you'd be up before I went to school. An' I gotta leave in ten minutes, so you'd better hurry!"

Before he could reply, Flynn heard quick footsteps coming up the stairs.

"Lewis William McMaster! You'd better not be—" Sara was hissing the words as she came to a halt in the doorway. Her gaze skated right over her son and collided with Flynn's.

He smiled at her, realizing now exactly why he felt so good. Her cheeks were flushed. Her short dark hair was tousled. She was wearing jeans and a sweater and a scowl—definitely well armored—but he remembered her curves and the softness of her, under the thin cotton of her nightgown.

The truth was he remembered a whole hell of a lot more than that from six years ago. And he knew he wanted it again. Wanted Sara again. Badly.

But he probably shouldn't let himself think about it too intently—not if he wanted to get out of bed anytime soon.

"Liam! I told you—"

"He was awake, Ma," Liam protested. "I didn't wake him up. Did I?" He turned to Flynn, his expression imploring.

Flynn shook his head, his eyes still on Sara. "He didn't wake me up."

"But he's gotta get up," Liam said urgently, "or he won't be able to come to school with me."

"Don't be ridiculous. He doesn't need to go to school with you." Sara stood, hands on hips, glowering at Liam. Flynn thought she looked gorgeous.

"It's show 'n' tell," Liam wailed. "I'm not gonna take my stupid dump truck I built with Legos when I got a father nobody's ever seen!"

"I'll go with him." Flynn started to throw back the covers, then thought better of it. "Go on down with your mom now," he said to Liam. "Let me get dressed. I don't suppose you have a razor?" he said to Sara.

"Disposable ones in the drawer in the cabinet in the bathroom. Not what you're used to, I'm sure. Extra toothbrushes, too." She didn't look at him, and she didn't look pleased, either.

"Come on, Liam," she said impatiently, and she reached out and grabbed his hand when he got close enough so she could tug him out the door. "You don't have to go with him," she said over her shoulder.

"Yes," said Flynn. He knew it in his bones. "I do."

Because he needed to. Because he wanted to be part of this family. He wanted Sara, yes. In his bed, yes. But more than just in his bed.

In his life.

CHAPTER SIX

THERE was no justice in the world.

Flynn Murray, even stubble-jawed and tousled, looked disgustingly refreshed and rested, while Sara, gritty-eyed and decidedly unrested, felt as if she'd been run over by a snowplow.

It was what came of lying awake most of the night.

But how on earth was she supposed to have slept?

Flynn might have had enough jet lag to knock him out like a light. But she wasn't so lucky.

She was still wired from everything that had happened that day—right from the moment she'd opened the door to find him there, to his encounter with his son, to the mind-blowing revelations he had made in the darkness before Liam had woken up.

All that alone would have been enough to keep her awake for hours. But then she'd ended up in her bed in Flynn's arms!

Sleep?

Not in this lifetime!

She'd barely closed her eyes. He might be snoring and unconscious, but she had been supremely conscious of the heat of his body pressed hard against hers. She had shifted slightly to see if he would wake—or if he'd been merely faking it—but he hadn't moved, except to breathe more deeply and settle more firmly against her. His arm snugged her closer. His breath tickled the hair against her ear.

How was she supposed to sleep like that?

She didn't think any woman would be able to sleep tucked hard against Flynn Murray, with him holding her tight.

She couldn't. Her mind spun. Her body hummed with awareness. She wanted—Dear God, she didn't know what she wanted!

She knew what she *shouldn't* want!

She had no doubt at all about that. But as she lay there in Flynn's arms, traitorous thoughts kept creeping in. They were foolish silly thoughts. Airy-fairy, happy-ending thoughts. Idealistic thoughts—ones that the young innocent Sara McMaster had once entertained.

But not this Sara, she reminded herself. This Sara knew better. This Sara was a realist. And dreams—even waking ones—about a happy ending with Flynn Murray were not realistic.

Even less realistic now than before, she reminded herself, because now he wasn't simply a peripatetic young journalist out to write a name for himself.

Now he was an earl.

She was sleeping with an earl.

Well, not exactly sleeping—though he was—but she was in bed with an earl. How unlikely was that?

She felt as if her whole world had been turned upside down. She'd finally psyched herself up to date Adam—to move out of limbo, to forget the past.

And now here she was, wrapped in the past's embrace.

He was asleep, though.

She could have slipped away then.

But she'd been cold and he was warm. And it was true what he'd said, there had been no place to go except the too-short sofa, and what if Liam woke up again and looked for her?

All manner of arguments had arisen in her mind—and every

one of them, damn it, had offered reasons for her to stay right where she was. It was foolish to do so.

But it was only one night, she told herself. One night to confront the past and get over it. She might as well be comfortable and warm while she did it.

She had shifted in his arms then, half-expecting that he would wake up. But he was deeply asleep, and she was able to roll onto her back and then turn further so that she lay facing him, her knee sliding between his, his leg trapping her right where she'd turned.

But here she could study him in the light reflected off the snow outside the windows. Could drink him in, looking her fill. In sleep he looked younger, more like he had when she'd met him. The lines bracketing his mouth had softened, his lips were parted, curved in a slight smile.

She wanted to touch them. Maybe if she did, she would learn to resist the effect they had on her. Because she was going to have to. They weren't going to spend however many nights he was here visiting in her bed. This was a one-off.

Yes, he would be part of Liam's life now and, peripherally, she supposed, part of hers. But just as they had six years ago, now too they inhabited two different worlds.

He was the earl of Dunmorey—the ninth earl of Dunmorey. He lived in a castle in Ireland, for heaven's sake! And she lived in the small story-and-a-half bungalow in Elmer, Montana, that her great-grandfather, Artie, had bequeathed her. "It's yours," he'd told her the day before he died. "So you can always do what you want and know you've got a roof over your head."

Definitely two different worlds, Sara thought, closing her eyes and trying not to think about who was holding her.

Maybe that was when she'd slept.

It was just past 5 a.m. when she jerked away. Jerked away

because though Flynn was still fast asleep, he had rolled onto his back and hauled her with him!

Now she was lying on top of him, her cheek against his chest, while his arm was draped loosely across her back.

Just like last time.

Just like the night they'd made love. The very last time he had taken her, Flynn had drawn her on top of him and had encouraged her to take the lead. "Your turn," he'd said, in that soft sexy voice. "Do what you want, Sar'."

And she had. She had explored his body, had touched and tasted, had learned what made him grip the sheets in his fists, what made him arch his back, what made him grit his teeth and say, "Damn it, Sara, you're killing me," before she slowly eased her body around his, before she took him in.

He had shattered then—and she had shattered with him. And had fallen asleep on his chest, cradled in the warmth of his arms.

And she remembered it all now so vividly that she felt as if her heart would burst through her chest. She remembered how wonderful it had been. And how cold and empty she'd felt after he had gone.

There was enormous temptation to stay there now, to recapture the joy of those brief moments, to rest her head against his chest, to listen to the steady thump of his heart.

But she didn't—because even in the darkness before the light of day she was a realist now. And Sara knew better than to stay with temptation too long.

So, quietly, she'd slipped out of the warm bed into the cold room. She was glad it was cold, she told herself, grabbing her clothes from the hook on the closet door and hurrying into the bathroom to get dressed. It made reality easier to bear. And as long as she didn't pause to look at Flynn still sleeping soundly, she'd cope.

Of course she would.

By the time she had to wake up Liam at seven-thirty, she had finished the bookwork for the hardware store she'd had to leave undone yesterday. She'd made his lunch. She'd done a load of laundry, fed the cat, done all the things she normally did.

She had her life back under control.

And if she'd assiduously avoided even glancing at the bedroom door she'd shut behind her when she crept out after waking Liam, what difference did it make? She knew Flynn was there.

It wasn't as if she were pretending otherwise.

Unfortunately, Liam knew it, too. And he wanted to dash in first thing and wake Flynn up.

Sara wouldn't let him. She'd shooed him past the door, threatened dire things if he woke Flynn up, and tried to keep him busy downstairs until it was time for school. But when she'd gone to the basement to put the washing into the dryer, she forgot to say, "Do *not* go upstairs."

And so, of course, Liam had.

And when she came back up and discovered his absence from the kitchen, there had been no question about where to look. She'd just hoped she wasn't too late.

Of course she had been.

And so she'd come face-to-face with Flynn, grinning and stretching and far too handsome for his own good. Or her good, more to the point. Sara felt all her hard-won resolution to resist him threaten to desert her then and there.

Fortunately, she wasn't quite the ninny she'd been at nineteen. She'd behaved—if not with quite the sangfroid she would have wished—at least with polite dismissive behavior. So what if she had lain in his arms all night?

Nothing had happened.

And nothing would.

And if she'd hustled Liam downstairs quickly, it wasn't because she was afraid of her feelings. It was because Liam needed to get his jacket and boots on and put his truck in his backpack for show-and-tell. It was nearly time to go to school.

"I'm not takin' my truck," Liam protested. "I'm takin' my dad."

"Don't be silly, Liam. He's still in bed. Besides, your truck is a wonderful thing to take. And you made it yourself."

"A dad's better," Liam said stubbornly, and clutched his backpack against his chest.

Sara would have argued with him, but she heard the thud of footsteps coming quickly down the stairs. Abruptly she turned and began scrubbing out the oatmeal bowls.

"All set." Flynn's voice was cheerful and upbeat. Turning, she saw that he was dressed in the same jeans and shirt and sweater he'd worn yesterday. Since he hadn't brought his luggage in, he'd had no choice. But his unruly hair was damp and combed, though his jaw was still dark with whiskery stubble, which made him look both piratical and sexy as all get-out.

Sara grimaced.

Flynn rubbed a hand over his jaw, misunderstanding—thank God—her expression. "I know. I found the razors. But I didn't have time. I'll shave when I get back. The kids won't care."

And the teacher will drool on your shoe tops, Sara thought, clenching the dish-washing sponge in her fingers. And just wait they found out he was an earl! "You don't have to go with him."

But Flynn was grinning and looked as if he relished the whole idea. "Of course I do. How many kids get to bring their long-lost dads to show-and-tell?"

He probably would relish it, Sara thought. He never minded the spotlight. Not even if it brought renewed focus on her youthful indiscretion with him. After all, he didn't have to live here.

Now he shrugged into his jacket as Liam hopped from one

foot to the other in gleeful anticipation. "I'll be back in a while."
He opened the door.

Liam, pausing only to give her a smacking kiss, scampered
out ahead of him. "Bye, Mom!"

"Bye."

"Bye, Sar'. *Slán leat.*" "Goodbye" in Irish. He'd taught her
that six years ago. But foolishly she hadn't thought he'd meant
it then. Now she wished he did.

"Goodbye," she said gruffly, turning back to the dishes,
willing him out the door.

But instead of leaving, he crossed the room and spun her
away from the sink and into his arms, wrapped them around her.

"Flynn!" she protested.

"Sara," he murmured, a wicked grin on his face. And then his
mouth swooped down and he kissed her with as much enthusiasm
and far more effect than Liam had.

Her brain buzzed. Her body melted. Her sanity scattered. She
tasted toothpaste and warm hungry male—one particular male.
She felt the rasp of his whiskers against her cheek. She clung to
him, all her control shattered. No fair! No fair!

What was he trying to do to her?

"Dad! C'mon!" Liam's voice drifted back from outside, impatient now. And when the kiss still went on, the door banged open.

Sara's eyes flew open to see Liam staring at them in amazement from the door. His eyes were like dinner plates. His
mouth like an *O*. And then a grin split his face. "Wow," he
breathed. "Oh, wow."

Oh, whoa, Sara thought. Oh, no!

She squirmed and finally twisted out of Flynn's embrace. Her
heart was pounding. Her face was flaming. She was furious, and
Flynn was grinning from ear to ear.

"I've missed you, Sara," he said.

Resolutely she shook her head. "Well, I haven't missed you! And I do not want you giving Liam ideas," she added through her teeth.

Although one look at their son told her it was far too late for that. She could almost see the wheels spinning in Liam's head.

And when Flynn followed him out, she heard Liam say, "Does that mean you're gonna marry my mom?"

Great minds, Flynn decided, thought alike.

Marrying Sara was the best idea he'd had in ages. And the fact that Liam had it too, and was obviously in favor of it—they'd discussed it on the way up the hill to school—made it a definite winner.

Not that he told Liam that. He just said it was definitely something to think about. And he asked what Liam thought.

Liam said he could use a father. Someone to build snow castles with and make forts with. And someone to keep his mom from being lonely.

"Is she lonely?" Flynn asked.

"Not when I'm home," Liam said. "But I can't be home all the time. Sometimes I play with my friends. And I go on sleepovers. She's lonely then. She says Sid's enough, but I don't think so."

"Sid?" There was another man in her life besides the cowboy?

"The cat."

"Oh, right." Flynn was surprised how relieved he was to discover that the main man in Sara's life had four paws and purred. He wanted to make Sara purr.

"If you got married, you could stay home with her," Liam said as they climbed the steps into the school building. "And," he added hopefully, "maybe we could visit Dunmorey."

It sounded like a good idea to Flynn.

Staying home at night with Sara would certainly be no hardship. Nor would building forts and snow castles with his son. He'd relished the time he'd spent with Liam so far.

And Sara? Well, they hadn't had much time—but then, they never had. Still, they could start. She was the mother of his son. And despite her resistance, despite her edginess and her prickly behavior, he was sure she was still Sara underneath. She sure as hell kissed like Sara!

It was a good thing Liam had come back in the door or he'd have forgotten all about being in show-and-tell at kindergarten.

"We'll discuss it," he promised Liam and followed his son into the school building.

Sara had the accounts from Taggart Jones's and Noah Tanner's bull-and-bronc-riding school all over the kitchen table. She'd spread them out as soon as the door had banged behind Liam and Flynn.

She refused to think about the kiss Flynn had given her. Refused to even acknowledge Liam's tactless question to his father as they went out the door. This was her work time. She had things to do, accounts to finish. Yesterday had been a lost day. She needed to get her act together.

But she hadn't managed much in the hour and a half she had between when Flynn and Liam left and when she heard the back doors rattle open and Flynn appeared in the room.

He was, of course, grinning broadly, looking inordinately pleased with himself.

"Sure an' I'm the hit of the Elmer kindergarten class," he announced in his best stereotypical heavy Irish brogue.

"Sure you are," Sara muttered, determined to ignore him. If she did, she had decided, he would leave her in peace, go back home. Go away!

So she spared him only a brief glance before going back to the column of figures she was clicking her way through on her calculator. She knew she would have to do it over later. Her brain around Flynn was far too irresponsible.

"It was fun. I got to show 'em Ireland on the map and point out where Dunmorey was," he went on cheerfully. "They were impressed by the castle."

"I can't imagine why," Sara said dryly.

He laughed. "Nor can I. It's a moldering pile of rocks. A demanding moldering pile of rocks."

Sara doubted that. She shrugged. "I'm working," she informed him, in case it wasn't completely clear.

"I can see that you are." His voice was solemn. His tone was not. She shot him a quick look to see a twinkle of amusement in his eyes.

"You're bothering me," she said.

"Am I? Good." And instead of apologizing and leaving, he took off his jacket and leaned back against the counter, smiling at her.

"It isn't good," she said in clipped tones. "I have work to do."

"I can wait. I'll go out to my car and get my laptop."

"No!"

"Well, if you're busy—"

"All right, fine," she said. "I won't be able to get any work done with you here."

"Fine. Let's talk," Flynn said.

"About what? Liam?"

"Liam," he agreed. "And other things." He started to grab one of the kitchen chairs, but then grabbed her hand instead, pulling her to her feet.

Sara tried to tug her hand out of his, but he wouldn't let go. He drew her with him towards the living room. "What other things?" she demanded.

"Us." He slipped his arms around her.

Her stomach clenched. She tried to pull away, but he held her close. "There is no us!" she protested.

"Is there not, Sara, *a stór*?" His eyes bored down into hers. His lips were a fraction from hers. Instinctively she wetted her own.

But he didn't kiss her. He steered her to the sofa where they'd sat last night. He didn't expect her to sit there with him again, did he? And *talk*?

As he turned, she took advantage of his bad leg and momentary imbalance to duck around him to get to her grandfather's old rocking chair.

But he was faster on his feet than she'd thought and he snagged her back, tumbling them both onto the sofa where she landed on top of him, looking straight into those mesmerizing eyes. They regarded her slumberously and far too sexily. How *did* he do that?

She scrambled to sit up, but he had hold of her hand. If there was no retreating to the rocking chair, at least she got to her back-against-the-sofa position she'd held last night. And then she answered his question. "No," she said fiercely. "There is not an 'us'!"

"And the kisses?" he probed, cocking his head, watching her, his fingers still laced with hers.

She pulled them out of his and hunched her shoulders, looking away. "No big deal."

"Liar." His voice was soft, but definitely challenging. "They are a very big deal. Need me to prove it?"

She glared at him furiously. "No, I don't need you to prove it. What do you want me to say? That you can turn me to putty? That I melt in your arms?" Even now, being this close to him— her knee touching the hard warmth of his thigh—her body wanted things her brain resisted.

His mouth quirked into a grin. "Well, I wouldn't mind hearing it."

"Consider it said." She bit the words out. "But it doesn't make any difference, Flynn. It doesn't matter. It was brief. It was meaningless. It's over."

"It's not over." The smile was gone. "Why are you fighting

it, Sar'?" he demanded, leaning closer. His voice had a rough edge to it. "Why are you fighting *me*?"

"Because I don't trust you! I don't know you. I thought I did— I thought you were the one person in the world who understood me, who would be there for me, who loved me—and I was wrong!"

There. He'd asked. She'd told him.

She couldn't get much clearer than that. She knotted her fingers together and turned her head, stared unseeing out the window. But out of the corner of her eye she could see his own hands. Saw him crack his knuckles. Heard him let out a harsh breath.

Then, "Maybe I'm the one who was wrong," he said quietly.

His words made her look over at him. Maybe he was wrong? About what? She couldn't ask. She waited for him to explain.

He didn't say anything for a moment. Then he did, speaking quickly. "I did what I thought was best, Sar'. Maybe I was wrong. Obviously, you thought I was. I can't change it. But I can do something now."

She tilted her head. "What do you mean?"

"You're upset because I wasn't there for you then. Fair enough. Now I can be. Now I will be," he amended.

She just stared at him.

He nodded, as if he'd made up his mind, then smiled at her, confident now. "We can tie the knot."

"What?"

"Get married."

"Don't be ridiculous. You don't want to marry me."

"I do." It sounded so like a vow she wanted to put her hands over her ears.

"No, you don't! You want Liam. And Liam thinks you should marry me."

"He does, in fact," Flynn said, and grinned as if Liam's suggestion made it all perfectly reasonable.

"He's *five,* Flynn! You don't let a five-year-old tell you who to marry!" She jumped up and slapped her hands on her hips, looking at him indignantly.

"I'm not doing it only for him," he protested, standing, too.

"I suppose you imagine that you're doing me a favor, too?" Sara spat.

"I'd be doing us all a favor. We're not indifferent to each other, Sara!"

They certainly weren't. She wanted to kill him.

She took a breath, tried for calm. Tried for some "indifference." And when she had got as close as she could, she slowly shook her head.

"No," she said. "Thank you," she added, though the words were dry and bitter in her mouth and she hardly felt thanks were in order. "Thank you for your very eloquent proposal. But I will not marry you."

Because, by God, lack of indifference on his part, complete hormonal meltdown on hers, and a five-year-old's blessing were not sufficient reasons to, as Flynn had so eloquently put it, "tie the knot."

For a man who made his living with words, Flynn thought, he had sure as hell made a mess of the ones he'd used to propose marriage.

But hearts-and-flowers were hard to come by between here and Elmer Elementary School, he thought as he stood out in the snow, trying to come to terms with his colossal screwup. Trying to figure out how to get it right.

He could hardly proclaim undying love, could he, when he'd only been back a day?

But, damn it, there was something—besides Liam— between them.

He'd felt it six years ago when Sara had knocked the breath

out of him. He felt it again now. Then he'd been too stupid to recognize it.

Maybe, let's be honest, he'd been afraid of it. Maybe he'd grabbed Sara's determined goals as a reason for leaving. But even if he'd wanted to marry her then, the truth was, he hadn't had much to offer her—a fledgling journalism career about to take a turn for the dangerous. A life of traveling wherever his stories took him. He had been a man on the move with no place to call home.

And Sara had been all about home. She might not have known it then, and he might not have been able to verbalize it—God, he really was bad with words when they mattered!—but it was true.

As different as she'd been from her family—her amazing mother, her tough, caring grandmother, her crazy siblings—she was still a part of the whole warm welcoming household. They sustained and supported her. She might live in contrast to them sometimes, but they had made her who she was.

Just as Dunmorey had made him who he was—a man on the move, a man who'd begun by rejecting expectations he couldn't live with, and now a man determined to prove his father wrong.

But he was more than that, too. He was a man with a son he wanted to be a father to.

And a man who'd just botched a marriage proposal to the woman who had stolen her way into his heart.

What heart?

A lot of people had asked that question over the years. And it was a fair one, Flynn had to admit.

He was well-known in journalistic circles for getting deep inside his subjects—and personally keeping everyone at arm's length. But why wouldn't he? After all, when the first experiences you could remember were of your father telling you that you didn't measure up, you learned not to care.

"Can't you get anything right?" his father had said furiously more often than Flynn wanted to remember. It had been the mantra of his youth. He could almost hear the old man saying it again now.

"I can get it right," he said fiercely to the old man, to himself and to anyone else who happened to be passing Sara's snow-covered garden. He hadn't wanted to get married. He'd dismissed his mother's determined attempts to get him a suitable wife—not that it had stopped her.

"I'm not interested," he'd told her.

"You will be," she'd said, "when the right one comes along."

Well, the right one had. Sara had.

And he wasn't going to walk away again from the one good thing that had ever happened to him.

That should have been the end of it.

But though Sara had made her dramatic exit, Flynn didn't leave. Oh, he went outside, and she dared hope. But, as she peeked through the kitchen curtains, he stood in the garden, kicked at the snow, then paced around, jammed his hands in his pockets and still looked, heaven help her, like the sexiest man on earth.

She was hopeless. Absolutely hopeless.

"Go away," she told him though she knew he couldn't hear her. Sid came up and head butted her shin. "He wanted to marry me," she told the cat. "Because we're not indifferent to each other."

She didn't know whether to laugh or cry. So she did what her mother would have suggested had Polly been here—she got to work.

He came back when Liam came home from school. She didn't know where he'd gone in the meantime. She didn't care.

She wished he'd already left, but she supposed it made sense to wait until Liam came home. He'd need to explain to Liam that he had to go.

But when Liam came in to sling his backpack on the chair and give her a hug, it wasn't to look crestfallen about his father's departure, it was to say he wanted to take Flynn to grandma and grandpa's to see his colt.

"What?" Sara still had her arms around him, but she looked over his head at Flynn who was standing inside the door. "You're leaving," she said.

"Just to Grandma's," Liam said pulling back and correcting her assumption. "To see Blaze. Dad says his brother is gettin' a horse. A stud." Liam turned to look at his father to make sure he'd got the right word.

Flynn nodded. "A stallion." He lounged against the counter, seeming perfectly at ease now. He certainly didn't look as if he had just proposed marriage to her—and been turned down. So apparently, despite his eloquent words, he was reasonably indifferent.

"I know what a stud is," she said. "I thought you'd be leaving."

"Just to Grandma's," Liam persisted, as if he couldn't believe his mother was so obtuse.

"I'm not leaving," Flynn said, and his eyes met hers, clear and direct and determined.

Which meant what?

Nothing, Sara assured herself, beyond the fact that he was staying to spend some time with Liam. Absolutely nothing to do with her.

"Fine," she said dismissively. "Go. But don't—" she looked at Liam "—eat so much you spoil your dinner."

She didn't want Flynn out there. Didn't want him establishing any sort of connection with her family. But she didn't see any way to prevent it with Liam having made the request. So she did the next best thing when they'd left. She rang her grandmother and told her they were coming.

"He's back?" Joyce said.

"Just to see Liam," Sara insisted. She had no intention of mentioning his proposal. "He wants to be a father to his son."

Joyce made a harumphing sound. "About time."

"Yes, well, apparently he didn't know." Sara repeated the saga of the letter following him all over the world.

"If you say so," Joyce said when she had finished.

"It's true." Sara didn't doubt that. "And, I think he's good for Liam."

"He'd better be," Joyce said fiercely, "or he'll be sorry he ever came back. And what about you, Sara? Is he good for you?"

"I'm fine," Sara lied.

If she said it often enough, though, she was determined it would be the truth.

"What can I do for you, baby?" Her grandmother obviously wasn't fooled.

"Just be polite," Sara said. "And, for Liam's sake, you probably shouldn't let Walt shoot him."

For her own sake, it might have been a blessing, because it seemed as if, far from making his excuses and leaving, Flynn was determined to stick around.

She succeeded in—mostly—putting him out of her mind while he and Liam were at the ranch.

But her grandmother rang after they'd left and said, "I'd forgotten what a charmer that man can be."

It wasn't what Sara wanted to hear. "Don't tell me he proposed to you," she said lightly.

"I'm married," her grandmother reminded her, then asked suspiciously, "did he propose to you?"

Sara didn't answer that.

"Did he see Blaze? What did he think?"

Her grandmother took the bait. "Oh, yes. Blaze was on his

best behavior. Flynn was impressed. He's impressed with that boy of his, too."

"Liam's mine."

"Of course he is, darling," Joyce said. "And he knows that. Says you've done a marvelous job with him. Had only good things to say about you."

"How nice of him." Sara clenched her teeth.

Her grandmother laughed. "I think he's a little bit smitten."

Sara didn't. She thought he was "not exactly indifferent." It was not the same thing.

"He was just being polite," she said. "I've got work to finish up before they get back," she told Joyce. "I'd better get going. Oh, by the way, did he mention when he was leaving?"

"No. Is he?"

"Of course he is."

Dear God, she hoped so.

But he certainly gave no sign of it. He came in with Liam when they got back. He took off his jacket and his boots and when she grudgingly offered a cup of coffee, he accepted.

"Is the Busy Bee still the only place to eat in town?" he asked.

She nodded.

"Then let's go there for dinner."

"Yea, let's!" Liam was all for it.

"You and Liam can—"

"All of us," Flynn said firmly.

She glared at him. He looked back impassively, waiting for her answer.

She shrugged irritably. "Whatever. But go away now. I've still got work to do."

He and Liam went upstairs. She could hear Liam chattering away, could hear Flynn's occasional more-measured tones.

She tried to work. By saying the figures out loud as she stabbed them in, she managed to keep on task. But it was almost a relief when, an hour later, Liam clattered down the stairs and came into the kitchen.

"Me an' Dad are starvin'."

They went to the Busy Bee. It was, as always, full of locals—cowboys and shopkeepers, Carol from the grocery, Loney from the welding shop, the elder Joneses back from Bozeman.

If everyone in Elmer didn't already know that Flynn Murray was back before the meal—which thanks to Liam almost everyone did—by the end of it, Sara was sure his presence in town was common knowledge. And apparently they all remembered him from when he'd come to report on the cowboy auction. Though really she knew they remembered that he'd left a child in their midst.

Everyone dropped by their table to say hello, to check him out, to be told by Liam, "This is my dad."

And Flynn, damn him, charmed them all. He shook their hands, asked about their families, their cattle, the weather, chatting easily, his hand on Liam's shoulder all the while and his knee pressed against hers under the table.

"Glad you're back," everyone said one way or another. "A boy needs his father."

"He does," Flynn agreed. "And I need my son."

"And Sara needs—" several began.

Sara, fortunately, always managed to cut off those suggestions before they left anyone's mouth. She'd never interrupted so many people in her life.

"It's been lovely to see you again," she said determinedly and looked towards the door hopefully.

"Ah, right." They nodded and nudged each other, and she realized she was giving the completely wrong impression.

By the time they got to dessert, Sara thought Flynn could have run for mayor—and won.

When they got home, she was hot, even in the frigid air, was frazzled and had had enough.

"I don't know what you think you're doing." She rounded on him the minute she'd sent Liam up to take a shower.

"You don't?" He sounded surprised. "I'm courting you."

She stared. "What?"

"Courting. Don't they use that term in America? It's when I come around and woo you, ask you out, bring you flowers and—"

"I know what the term means! Stop it!"

He shook his head, slowly and deliberately. "I blew it this afternoon, Sara. I'm not blowing it again."

"There is no again!"

He just looked at her and she knew he didn't believe a word she said.

"You are not spending the night here," she informed him.

He lifted a brow, as if assessing how serious she was. She was very serious indeed. She didn't need any determined-to-seduce Flynn Murray in her house—in her bed—another night.

"You can stay and say good-night to Liam. Then you leave. Promise me."

He studied her for a long moment, as if weighing her seriousness. Apparently he figured that she was very serious indeed, because after a long minute he nodded. "If that's what you think you need, Sara."

She didn't think it, she knew it.

"It's the way it is," she said sharply, and she turned and hurried upstairs to make sure Liam was getting on with his bath.

When he was finished and in bed, Flynn sat beside him and told him a story about Dunmorey castle and an earl who got stabbed defending it against the bad guys.

"He won, didn't he?" Liam's eyes shone eagerly. "He didn't die, did he?"

Flynn shook his head. "Of course he won. That's why we've still got the castle. And he lived to a ripe old age. Died in his bed with his boots on."

Liam giggled. "How come he wore his boots to bed?"

Flynn shrugged, a wry expression on his face. "Probably because the place was knee-deep in water."

"Really?" Liam's eyes got wide. "But I thought you said there wasn't a moat."

"There isn't. The roof leaks. Although, to be fair, it probably didn't in his day."

Liam settled back against the pillows and gave a little wriggle of contentment. "It sounds so cool. I wanta see it."

"Liam!" Sara said sharply. "It's time to go to sleep." And it was not time to talk about going to see any castles.

"But—"

"In time," Flynn promised. His eyes met Sara's, though, not Liam's. And while she read challenge in them, to her dismay she read *promise,* too. "Your mother's right. Time to go to sleep." He got off the bed and leaned down awkwardly to give his son a kiss. "Go to sleep now."

"But—"

"Sleep," Flynn said firmly before Sara could, which annoyed her further, because Liam would have argued with her, but he settled in without another word when Flynn told him to.

She glared wordlessly at Flynn who gave her a bland look in return. So finally she simply bent and kissed Liam good-night, then waited for Flynn to precede her out the door.

"You need to go now," she said when they got downstairs. "I have work to do."

He drummed his fingers on the countertop for a moment, as if deciding whether to argue with her or not.

"You promised." There was a look in his eyes—a determined-to-seduce look that made her hold her ground and meet his gaze with a steely no-nonsense one of her own. Though she knew if he walked into the living room and sat down, she couldn't throw him out.

Finally he shrugged lightly. "Whatever you say, Sar'." He snagged his jacket off the hook by the door and slipped it on. "See you in the morning."

She shook her head. "No, you won't. I have work to do. Liam's in school."

"We can both work."

She snorted. "Doing what?"

"My book. Estate business." He shrugged. "I've got plenty to do. I'm not one of the idle rich, believe me."

"You have a castle."

He laughed humorlessly. "Not exactly a money-making proposition. More of an albatross. A responsibility."

"Like Liam."

"Not at all like Liam." He moved closer, his eyes boring into hers. Her own went to his mouth, remembering the last time he'd looked at her that way.

Quickly Sara took a step back. But it was too late. Flynn reached for her, slid his arms around her and drew her hard against him.

"Flynn!"

"I'll go," he said. "But not yet. I'm courting." And he bent his head and touched his lips to hers.

Sara went still. Resisted. She fought his touch, his taste with every bit of determination that she could muster.

It didn't work. There was a gentle persuasiveness to his kiss. It didn't demand or assert. It asked. It promised.

He kissed her with hunger, with passion, and yet with the assurance that she could take as long as she wanted to come around. He would still be here, kissing her, as if he had all the time in the world.

And damn it, she tried. She tried so hard to remain indifferent. To tune him out, turn him off. And she couldn't do it.

The kiss went on. And on. He touched her lips, stroked them lightly with his tongue. Pressed butterfly kisses to her cheeks, her eyelids, her jaw. His breath caressed her, made her weak, fed her hunger, shattered her resolve.

She could fight him. She couldn't fight herself. She couldn't turn her back on the surge of passions and emotions that for six years she had tried to pretend didn't exist.

She kissed him back. She couldn't help it.

She was her own worst enemy.

She opened her lips under the teasing temptation of his. She welcomed the nibble of his teeth, the flick of his tongue. She sighed and heard him groan, felt the heat of his body as it pressed against hers. Trapped between him and the door, she should have pushed him away. But nothing in her wanted to do it.

She needed to stop this. Call a halt. Push him away. Everything rational in her told her that. And the traitorous hungry Sara who had missed him and loved him wouldn't let her. It said "Later. Just a few more seconds. Just a taste. Just a touch. Just a little longer."

Until at last it was Flynn who stepped back, who pulled away.

He dragged his mouth from hers and set her away from him, breathing hard, his voice ragged as he said, "We do still have it, Sara." His mouth twisted. "If you see what I mean."

She stared at him, stunned and shaken, her tender mouth a silent *O*, her heart slamming against her chest. Would she have stopped if he hadn't?

Would she?

He opened the door, his gaze never leaving hers. "I'll be back in the morning, Sar'. *Coladh sámh.*"

Sara blinked. "*Coladh sámh?*" she repeated dazedly.

Flynn's mouth twisted wryly. "Sweet dreams."

CHAPTER SEVEN

SWEET dreams?

He ought to have his head examined. His own were highly charged, erotic, and frustrating as hell, which probably served him right.

What kind of idiot broke off a kiss when the woman he was wooing had finally started kissing him back?

This one. Flynn Murray.

Because it had seemed like a smart idea at the time. And because he'd given her his word.

As much has he would have loved to have swept her off her feet and up to her bedroom to make love to her, he couldn't. The time wasn't right. Not now. Now yet.

It would be marvelous and sexy and he was certain he could make it good for her. It would also blow up in his face.

Sara valued promises. Integrity. Keeping your word. And while he might have been able to subvert her resolve in the short run, there would be recriminations, angst and remorse after.

If he had taken her up to her room and made love to her, she would have hated him more in the morning than she was already trying to hate him now—and with far better reason.

So, he'd left. He'd kept his word.

The mistake might have been kissing her goodbye to make

sure she thought of him after he left. He hoped she had, because he had certainly suffered the plight of the terminally frustrated thereafter.

Flynn wasn't used to thinking in terms of the *L* word, but he sure as hell didn't know what else you would call the sort of martyrdom that had had him stopping the car and throwing himself into a snow bank instead of throwing Sara onto a bed and giving them both what they really wanted.

So he dreamed of her—and of fulfillment.

And he awoke denied, and more frustrated—and determined—than ever.

He was up and at the grocery store at six. He hit the florist shop as soon as he saw the light on. And he showed up on Sara's doorstep at eight-thirty, bearing his laptop, groceries, a book and flowers.

"For you," he said, handing her the bouquet. They were daffodils, bright and sunny yellow, shouting of spring in the midst of a Montana winter. "When I saw them, I thought of you." She always looked like spring to him.

Even this morning with her eyes slightly bloodshot, her hair tousled, and her face pale—from lack of sleep, he dared hope—she was the bright spot in his life.

Her eyes widened when he thrust the flowers into her hands. But she didn't speak. She just stood there, holding the damn daffodils in nerveless finger, staring at him.

"I'm not kidding," he said irritably, when no enthusiastic thanks, no smiles, no gushing were forthcoming. "They remind me of sunshine. So do you."

At her startled blink, he grimaced. "More eloquence," he muttered. "God help me."

But then she grinned—and it was such a delighted, delightful grin that the sun really did seem to come out. "Thank you," she said. "They're lovely."

And the brightness in her eyes told him she meant it.

"Dad! You're back!" Another bit of brightness—albeit a moving one—as Liam hurtled down the stairs and flung himself at Flynn. His son was still wearing a pajama top with his jeans, he had only socks on his feet, and his hair wasn't combed. "Guess what Mom did! She slept through her alarm!"

"Did she?" Flynn couldn't help grinning at that. Had her night been as bad as his had been? He hoped so.

"It didn't go off," Sara mumbled, her back to him as she put the flowers in a bright-red glazed water pitcher and set them on the table.

"That happens," Flynn agreed happily.

She shot him a look. He shrugged, grinned again. She made a tiny irritated huffing sound, then turned to Liam. "Go put a shirt on. And your boots. You can't go to school in your pajamas!"

"I'm going. I'm going." Liam rolled his eyes, then grinned at Flynn, yanked his pajama top over his head and, waving it like a banner, raced back upstairs to get a shirt for school.

"And hurry!" Sara yelled after him. "What *is* this?" She demanded again as Flynn began unloading the bags onto the table.

"Amazingly enough, it's food." Which she could see if she looked. "I can't expect you to feed me without contributing."

"Who said I was going to feed you?"

He smiled. "Don't be churlish, Sara, *a stór*. It doesn't become you."

She narrowed her eyes at him, then raked a hand through her hair, mussing it the way he wished he could have mussed it last night. "I worked very late last night," she told him. "I'm tired. I have a lot to do today."

"Well, I won't bother you today. I'll be silent as a mouse."

"You're gonna stay?" Liam demanded, reappearing with his shirt on, though buttoned wrong. He was hastily redoing it as he looked to Flynn for an answer.

"Hoping to. Unless your mother kicks me out."

Both of them turned their gazes on Sara. The look she gave Flynn said, *You will be sorry.* But she sighed and told Liam, "He can stay."

"So you'll be here when I get home?" Liam pressed.

"I'll be here," Flynn promised.

"I don't know what you're going to do here all day," Sara grumbled after Liam finally left.

"Work, same as you." He unloaded the groceries, and though she muttered, she put them away. When he finished, he opened his briefcase and got out his laptop, then picked up something else, weighed it in his hand a moment, then turned and held it out.

"This is for you, too."

She shut the cupboard where she'd been putting the groceries and turned, putting out her hand. "What is—your book," she said staring at the hardback book in her hands and then at him.

Flynn felt far more nervous than he'd expected, giving it to her. He didn't care what anyone else thought of it. But Sara's opinion mattered.

"It's the third one I've written. They've all come out in Europe, but this is the first one to be published over here."

She was turning it over in her hands, studying the cover, the title, the picture of him on the back.

"It's not out yet, officially. Comes out in a couple of weeks. You're the first on your block to have one." He grinned, feeling oddly self-conscious, wondering if it had been a mistake. It had always been a mistake to show his father anything he'd done.

Sara opened it. Found the inscription on the title page where he'd signed it for her. He'd debated about what to say. Had finally scrawled the words in it this morning right before he'd left the motel. He didn't know if he'd done the right thing. Maybe he'd just made things worse.

"Sara," he'd written, "this is what I was doing when I should have been with you. I will be from now on. Love, Flynn."

She read his words in silence. Stared at them for far too long. Then she lifted her gaze and met his, hers was steady and serious.

"Thank you for the book." Her tone was quiet, almost formal, giving nothing away. Making no promises.

But he took heart. At least she didn't throw it at him.

Sara felt like she was under siege.

A very tempting sort of siege—complete with flowers and groceries one day, dark chocolate and darjeeling tea the next.

When Flynn Murray set out to get something—or in this case, someone—he obviously left no holds barred.

He was there every morning. He was there all day long. He worked hard. He paused to talk. He told her about places he'd been, people he'd met.

He told her about his book. She hadn't been able to resist reading it. She might have been more capable of resisting him, if she'd tried.

But she wanted to know about the places he'd been, the people he'd interviewed, the men who had shot him...

The night she read that part, she cried.

"It's a wonderful book," she told him. "You make these people so vivid. So real."

"They are real," he'd said. "I just wrote what I learned."

But he had written it so clearly, so descriptively, so well.

Which was why it seemed so strange when he talked about Dunmorey and his natural eloquence deserted him. Then he was left with stark silence, long pauses, and the barest words to manage what he wanted to say.

The castle's history, he could manage easily enough. The

tales of politics and perils, of feisty ladies and fierce earls came easily enough off his tongue.

But when he talked about recent times—about his childhood there, about his brothers—the flow of words nearly dried up.

He did talk a little about Will.

"He was a bloody hero," he'd told her raggedly one day. "Always did the right thing. Was always there for everybody. He'd have been a hell of a better earl than I'm being."

Sara doubted that was true.

She saw how hard he worked. He got a fair number of calls from his agent and his editor, from someone in publicity who was trying to set up a book tour for him, but mostly he had calls about Dunmorey.

He might be half a world away, but he was never far out of touch with what was happening with the tenants, the land, the farm, the new stable. Everything that was being done he had a hand in.

She caught only snatches of conversation, but she was impressed by how diligent he was, how committed, how much it mattered to him.

And when she commented on it, he shrugged. "Who else is going to do it? I'm the earl."

He was the earl.

Something else to think about.

But as the days went by and they worked on their respective jobs, she learned that he was still the Flynn she'd fallen for. And though she did her best to keep him at arm's length, he could stay at arm's length and still tease her, cajole her, charm her.

And the sneakiest part was that he did so in a way that was not overtly romantic. He never resorted to a big-time seduction. There were shared confidences, teasing grins, light touches. But there were no more deep passionate kisses. A look was all he needed to set her on fire. And the looks were still there.

He could smoulder for Ireland, she thought.

But it was as if he knew she had her guard up, that she could resist him if he tried to seduce her in the usual way.

So he didn't do it the usual way.

Instead he fixed her toaster. He changed her fuse. He shoveled the snow off her porch roof.

"You shouldn't be driving out in the middle of nowhere in the middle of winter by yourself," he'd objected when she'd told him that morning she was going out. He'd wanted to go with her.

But she had dismissed his concern. "I grew up in Montana. I'll be fine."

And she was, though it started to snow before she got back. The roads got bad, and going over the pass, she had to stop and put on her chains. So she was later than she expected.

Flynn and Liam were waiting at the door.

"We were worried," Liam told her. One look told her it wasn't Liam who'd been doing most of the worrying.

"You shouldn't have been." She shrugged off her jacket and bent to give him a hug. He wrapped his arms around her neck and gave her a fierce one in return. "I have a cell phone," she reassured him. "I'd have called if I'd had a problem."

"And we certainly could have done something about it from here," Flynn said sarcastically.

Sara looked up in surprise to see him glowering down at her. His dark hair was tousled, as though he'd run his hands through it. His voice was angry. A muscle in his jaw ticked.

She stood up again. "I would have called," she said again. "Really, I'm fine." She went so far as to reach out and give him a reassuring pat on the arm.

But the pat disappeared as he hauled her hard against him and held her tight.

He kissed her hard. Desperately, almost. The first kiss he'd given her since that night. She could feel his heart pounding against her chest.

"You'd better be fine," he said roughly. "You aren't doing that again."

"Of course I am. It's my job."

"Then I'm going with you."

She didn't argue with him. There was no point. He wasn't going to be here forever. They both knew that. He had a book tour coming up starting next Monday. His publicist was always calling with new strategies, new possibilities. And when those dried up, he had duties—plenty of them—back in Ireland.

They hadn't talked about it, but they both knew it was only a matter of time until he would be leaving. His visit here was just that—a visit—and it was drawing to a close.

When he was gone, she would do what she had always done.

"You scared me to death. Don't ever do that to me again," he said fiercely, his eyes alight with green fire.

"I was fine," she said for the third time.

"You might have been," he said heavily, shaking his head. "I wasn't."

She was going to be the death of him.

If not of frustration, then of worry. His reward, he guessed, was the way she began gradually to relax around him. She smiled more, was defensive less. She talked more, too—told him about Liam's babyhood, about her work, about the rest of her family. And she began to ask about his.

Flynn didn't mind telling her about his work. The writing was his joy. Though for Sara, he did gloss over some of the more gruesome things he'd seen and some of the grittier bits of his experience.

He was all right when he told her about Dunmorey, too—at

least the history and geography of it. He could tell her about the mad earl and the bad earl and all their various lascivious ladies. He did so with relish. And he went on and on about the gardens and the woods and the lake. It had, after all, been the Eden of his boyhood. Remembering that part of Dunmorey was a pleasure, even if it did lead him to talking about Will.

He told her about Will, about what a good brother he was.

"A saint, really," he said, his throat tight. "He could get along with everyone. Do everything." It was still hard to believe he was gone. Not that he didn't have constant reminders.

Every day—even in Montana—Flynn got phone calls about the estate, from Mrs. Upham and from Dooley, the farm manager. He dealt with them. But when the contractor for the stables and the bank financing the stables got into the act, "Direct your questions to my brother," he told them firmly.

Sometimes, like this afternoon, he found her looking up from her accounts and watching him, smiling when he got off the phone from the latest crisis.

"What?" he said as he hung up. "Something funny?"

Sara shook her head. "You really are the earl," she marveled.

"Yes," he said a little stiffly. It was all too reminiscent of his father's doubt. "Is that a problem?"

"Just a reflection. When you talk to your editor or agent or those publicity people—you're quick and witty and conversational. But when you do earl stuff, you use a completely different voice. Your Earl's Voice."

Flynn frowned. "My what?"

"Your voice. It goes all clipped and formal and authoritarian. Very 'not suffering fools gladly.' You stand up straighter, too. And you look down your nose." She slanted a grin at him. "Very impressive."

He gave her a mock scowl. "Is that so?"

She widened her eyes and nodded impishly. "And a little scary."

"Scary? We don't want that." He set his phone on the counter and came around the side of table. "We'd rather have you laughing than scared."

And then, because he couldn't help himself, because it had been far too long since he'd touched her and he wanted to every minute of every day, he hauled her to her feet and began tickling her.

She did laugh then, wriggling in his arms, making him hotter and hungrier for her than ever. His own laughter dried up in the heat of his desire. And it was a small step to sliding his arms around her, pulling her hard against him, and finally hungrily kissing her.

And almost at once he felt her response, felt her arms come around him, felt her lips open under his, her tongue touching his.

Neither of them were laughing now. They were all hands and mouths and bodies pressed tightly together. He tugged up her sweater to let his hands roam over the soft silken skin of her back. He felt his own shirttails dragged out of his jeans, knew the feel of her fingers as they slid up his spine, the simple touch making him quiver with need for her.

"Sara." He trailed kisses along her jaw and when her head dropped back, he trickled them lightly down to the base of her throat. His hands slid down her back and dipped beneath the waistband of her jeans, traced the edge of her panties, then slipped lower still, to knead the soft globes of her buttocks, to feel her press close against him. His heart pounded. His breathing quickened. He needed her now, needed to take her up to her room and get rid of all these restricting clothes and—

The door banged open. "I'm home!" Liam sang out. "Oh!"

"Liam!" His name was a gasp on Sara's lips.

She jerked her hands away from Flynn's back and stumbled out of his embrace. Her face flamed and her fingers fumbled as she frantically adjusted her sweater, trying to catch her breath and smile a welcome at their son over Flynn's shoulder at the same time.

Flynn didn't see Liam's reaction. Sara had been the one facing the door, not him. And even now he didn't turn around. Didn't dare. Left his shirttails out. Discretion and all that, though he doubted Liam would notice anything amiss.

Liam was five, not fifteen. He'd seen them kissing. Big deal. Well, not to a five-year-old.

But Flynn needed a minute. Hell, he needed a lifetime. His body was trembling. His breathing was coming in short shallow gulps. And he barely even had it under control when his phone rang for the twentieth time that day.

Sara grabbed it off the counter and thrust it into his hand. "Why don't you take the call in the living room," she suggested crisply, then turned to Liam. "So, how was school?"

Flynn expected Sara would freeze him out after that. He anticipated a return of the arctic chill she'd treated him to when he'd first arrived. But while she seemed to step back a little that evening, she didn't try to bite his head off or withdraw completely.

She was a bit quieter at dinner, contemplative almost. Distracted, perhaps.

While they were sitting in the living room after eating and Flynn built a fire in the fireplace, she just took up some mending and didn't say a word. It was, of course, barely noticeable because Liam never met a conversational lull that he couldn't fill.

Still, Flynn was aware of it. And worried about it, too.

After Liam went to bed, they came back downstairs. He considered apologizing. But he had nothing to apologize for, damn it—except for possibly scandalizing their son. There had been two people involved in that kiss. Two people who wanted it to happen. Not just him!

And he wasn't sorry he'd done it.

"Sara—"

"I'm a little tired tonight," she said, moving around the living room, straightening things up, instead of sitting down and picking up the jeans she had been patching. "I think I might go to bed early."

"Are you brushing me off?"

"No! I— No," she said more moderately. "I…just need a good night's sleep." She didn't look at him when she spoke. She was focused on lining up the magazines on the coffee table with military precision.

"Are you okay?" He wasn't apologizing, but he was concerned.

She nodded, her back still to him. "Of course. I have to be up early. It's getting closer to tax time. I have a lot of people coming in. The Joneses will be here in the morning." She turned long enough to give him a fleeting smile.

"All right," he said. "I'll shove off then."

He was tempted to go back and kiss her, to prove it wasn't a fluke what had happened between them.

He didn't, because somewhere in his life he really had learned patience. He would overcome. He would survive.

Eireoidh Linn.

His lips quirked at the appropriateness of the sentiment. Apparently he did have something in common with the earls of Dunmorey after all.

It wasn't a good night's sleep she needed, Sara thought, lying in her bed and staring at the ceiling.

It was Flynn.

The minute he walked out, she wished she'd called him back. She'd fought with herself all afternoon, all evening—ever since Liam had walked in the door and interrupted their kiss. She'd tried to understand what had happened, tried to think, to analyze, to rationalize.

But try what she would, there was only one conclusion. And there was no sense in lying to herself anymore.

She loved Flynn.

She supposed she always had. Her body was simply more honest than her brain. Braver, too. More willing to risk.

And after that kiss today—a kiss which she had wanted and had participated in every bit as much as he had—there was no way she could go on pretending she didn't care. If Liam hadn't come in just then, she knew exactly where they would have ended up. Right here in her bed.

They would have come upstairs together and followed their desire to its natural conclusion—and it would have been her choice as much as Flynn's.

Tomorrow they could. The thought danced through her mind, teasing her, tempting her. Daring her.

Yes, tomorrow they could!

She fell back onto her bed, hugging her pillow tight.

The bedside phone rang. She grabbed it. "Hello?"

"Hi. It's Flynn."

Of course it was. Her breath caught in her throat at the unexpected joy of hearing his voice. "I was just…thinking about you."

"I'm on my way to the airport."

"What?"

"All those phone calls today about the book tour… It was supposed to start Monday. My publisher just called. They got a slot open tomorrow on *US This Morning*. I'm it."

"But where is he?" Liam asked the next morning when he came down to find his mother alone in the kitchen.

"He had to go," she said, proud of herself for the cool dispassionate tone of her voice. "You knew he was leaving."

"But Monday!" Liam protested. "He said Monday!"

"Things change." Didn't they just? And wasn't she glad she hadn't made a fool of herself last night.

"When's he comin' back?"

Was he coming back?

Sara had thought he was six years ago. Would have bet her life on it. This time, of course, he'd insisted he would. He'd sworn up and down.

"It's not like last time, Sara," he'd said. "I've got the bloody tour, then I'll be there."

But she still felt as if she'd had the rug—or perhaps her whole world—pulled out from under her. Her own fault no doubt. But she couldn't help the feeling.

"Why'd he go?" Liam demanded. "Why didn't he say good-bye?"

Sara explained about the sudden open slot on a national television program, about him needing to take advantage of it, about barely being able to catch the last plane out.

And wasn't it lucky she'd wanted an early night? she thought humorlessly.

"Can I watch?" Liam demanded, already heading for the television.

Sara wanted to say no. She wanted to crawl back into bed and pull the covers over her head.

"Go ahead," she mumbled.

And because she was a masochist, she even went and watched with him. She stood there behind Liam, gripping the back of his chair, and watched as Flynn, bright-eyed even after what had to have been a sleepless night, and drop-dead gorgeous as always, charmed them all.

The interviewers, the audience, millions of viewers at home, no doubt, lapped up his wit, his humor, his smashing grin, twinkling eyes, unstoppable charm. He was the Flynn she'd fallen for all those years ago, flirting with the world the way he had once flirted with her.

"Is that all?" Liam demanded when the segment was over.

It was enough, Sara thought. "Yes," she said.

"But—"

"They only do short clips to give people a taste," she told Liam. "To whet their appetite."

She was sure the viewing public's appetite had been well and truly whetted. She personally didn't think she'd ever feel like eating again.

"What'd you think?"

"I—" She sounded shocked. As if she didn't expect his call. As if she thought she'd never hear from him again.

Think again, sweetheart, Flynn thought. He'd called her the minute he'd been able to get two minutes to himself. Had jammed himself into the only reasonably quiet space he could find after he left the studio. He'd only been off the air an hour. Less. But it seemed like forever since he'd talked to her on his way to the airport last night.

He hadn't wanted to leave. "Tomorrow?" He'd been aghast last night when the publicist had to tell him about the interview slot.

He'd just got back to motel, feeling edgy and worried about leaving Sara to have her "early night"—hoping it didn't mean she'd be mustering all her defenses—and when his mobile rang, he'd grabbed it, hoping against hope it would be her.

In his wildest dreams she'd be saying, "Come back. Let's finish what we started."

But it had been his publicist, Gary, saying, "I have great news!"

From a publicity standpoint, of course, it was. It was a coup to get him on the show. "Absolutely fantastic," Gary had said. "You can't buy exposure like this!"

Flynn had suggested alternative days. Next week.

"Tomorrow morning," Gary had said. "The only slot we'll ever see. Be there."

So he was here. But his heart was back in Elmer with Sara.

"Or didn't you watch?" he said now. Not that he wanted her answer to that. He thought he probably already knew it. And he was delighted when his fears weren't confirmed.

"I...we...watched."

So she'd told Liam. Maybe it was going to be okay. "Good. I was afraid you wouldn't. Figured you'd be ticked. You have a right to be," he said honestly.

"No."

A swift protest, which meant, he supposed, that she still didn't think she had any rights where he was concerned.

"Yes, you do," he said firmly. "I didn't want to come. But frankly, I didn't have a choice. There's a lot riding on this book. I need it to be a success. Not just for me—but for Dunmorey."

"Dunmorey?"

He'd told her a lot about Dunmorey, but not about how much money it took to keep it going. But that was his problem, no one else's. "There are a lot of things that need to be done," he said stiffly.

"Of course." Her voice was fading. Was it a bad connection or...?

"I'm only trying to explain why I needed to do this. I didn't want to go so suddenly. It shouldn't have been like that."

"You do what you need to do."

He was losing her. He could hear it in her voice. "Sara!"

"You were great," she said. "I have to go. The Joneses will be here any minute."

"I'll call you this afternoon. I'll talk to Liam. And you."

But she was already gone.

* * *

She didn't know what to think.

He called them every day. To talk to Liam, of course. But sometimes he called when Liam wasn't even there.

"He's at school," she always said impatiently. "You know that."

"I do," he replied unrepentantly, a smile in his voice. "I must have called to talk to you."

Of course they talked about Liam. Flynn wanted to know everything. And then he asked about Sid, about Celie and Jace, the rest of her family. And then he asked about her.

"I'm fine," she always said. "Busy, very busy." It was March now, tax season. It was absolutely true.

"I miss you," he told her.

"I—" But the words stuck in her throat. She'd had too many years of denying what she felt for him to find them easy to say. Her one night of honesty—cut out from under her almost immediately by his departure—didn't seem to extend very far.

"You can do it," he said.

"Can do what?"

"Say the words. Miss. You. They aren't hard. Come on. Try it." He was laughing.

She wanted to laugh. She wanted to cry. "Go away, Flynn Murray," she said. "I have work to do."

They kept him sane.

Liam, of course. But mostly Sara.

He never knew what city he was in, what show he was on, forgot almost at once who he was talking to because, though he did everything his publisher asked him to, his real focus was on Montana.

On a little boy in Montana that he couldn't imagine living without now.

And on the little boy's mother whom he wanted more than he wanted food or sleep or a *New York Times* bestseller—though it turned out he had one of those on his hands.

It was nice. More than nice. He was glad. But he was thinking more about Sara.

He missed her desperately. Told her so every time he called. She didn't say she missed him. She usually said, "I'll get Liam." Sometimes, though, he managed to call during the day when Liam was at school.

She acted impatient, but she didn't hang up. That was a plus. And if he asked about Liam, she usually began to talk to him. Of course she told him about Liam's activities first of all. But when he pressed a bit, asked the right questions, she told him what she'd been doing that day, too.

She told him about Sid's trip to the vet because he had a bad tooth. She told him about the truck that overturned on the highway to White Sulphur Springs. She told him that Sloan was in Rome and Polly, Daisy and Jack were going to go visit him.

He hung on every word. It made him feel as if he were there. With her.

To keep her on the phone, not because he gave a damn about any of it, Flynn told her about what he'd seen in San Francisco and Dallas and New Orleans and Chicago. He told her funny stories about things he'd seen and people he'd met just to hear her laugh. He missed her so damn much.

"I'll be back in four weeks," he said, and thought it sounded like forever. But then it was three weeks. Two weeks. And then, at last, it was one.

He began counting the days, the hours until he could get back. Began making plans.

His editor said the book had done so well they were doing yet another printing and wasn't that great. And it was, of course. But the best thing was that he was going to be back in Elmer in twenty-seven hours.

With Liam. And Sara.

And then his brother Dev called from Ireland.

"The bank is balking at the loan on the stables. They want more collateral. They want to see business plans."

"So show them," Flynn said. He'd been blessedly free of most Dunmorey worries while on tour. But now it felt like the other shoe, about to fall. "You've got everything we did." The plan had been Dev's primarily. Flynn's part had been to put up the castle as collateral.

"I have," Dev said. "But to go any further, they need to see more assets. They say there's too much debt. Dunmorey needs more revenue production. More avenues for income."

"Tell me something I don't know."

"They want to talk to you."

"So tell them to call me."

"In person," Dev said. "Friday."

"Like hell!"

"It won't go through otherwise," Dev said. There was more than a little desperation in his voice. "Doesn't matter that the earl of Dunmorey is backing me. They only want to talk about money, Flynn. We can make it back with this horse. I know we can. We've just got to get up and running. And that means talking to the bank again. Friday."

Flynn had planned on being in Elmer on Friday at long last, settling in for a spell, enjoying his son, courting Sara, convincing Sara.

"Friday," Dev said. "Or we're done without ever having a chance."

Flynn knew the feeling all too well.

* * *

"I have to go to Ireland."

They were in the airport, still collecting his bags, Liam hanging on his arm, Sara standing there, dazed at how her heart had leapt at the sight of him, then plummeted at his new revelation.

"But you just got here," Liam said, climbing up Flynn as if he were a tree.

"And I want you to come with me." He said it to both of them, but he was looking straight at her.

"Yea!" Liam cheered and threw his arms around his father's neck.

"What!" Sara was appalled, shaking her head. "When? No!"

"Yes. I have to go. Tomorrow. On Dunmorey business. And I don't want to go without you."

"Well, you're going to have to."

"Can we see the castle?" Liam was squirming in his arms between the two of them. "Can we?"

"We can," Flynn said.

"No," Sara said. "We cannot. It's tax season. I have commitments."

"But, Ma—"

Flynn set Liam down and pointed him in the direction of the luggage carousel. "Go see if my bag's there yet."

Liam opened his mouth to protest, then, seeing the look on his father's face, bobbed his head and scampered off to look for Flynn's baggage. Sara stayed where she was.

"I have to do this, Sara."

"Do it." She folded her arms across her chest. "Doesn't matter to me."

"It matters to me! You and Liam matter to me. I've been waiting all month to be with you again."

She just looked at him.

"They have phones in Ireland. Faxes. The Internet. You can talk to your clients, do their taxes."

"I don't want—"

"You're being selfish, Sara."

"I?" She stared at him, furious at the accusation.

"Do you remember what you told me the hardest part of your life was?" Flynn asked, making her blink in surprise.

Her eyes narrowed suspiciously. "What are you talking about?"

"Six years ago," he went on. "You took me up to see the ranch house where you'd lived when you were little. You showed me the swing your dad had hung in the tree. You showed me the tree house he built for you. Remember?"

Sara's throat tightened. She nodded.

"I remember, too. And you said the hardest part of your life was when your dad died and you couldn't have him there anymore. Do you remember that?"

The noise and bustle of the airport swirled around her, but she didn't hear or see it because yes, damn it, she remembered that, too.

She could still get a prickling feeling behind her eyes every time she thought about that swing, about the way she'd laughed when her dad had pushed her, about the tree house he'd built for her and her sisters. About how she'd carried the lumber for him and brought him the hammer and the nails when he'd asked. About how she'd followed him around and he'd called her "the best kid in the world."

She blinked rapidly, clenched her jaw tight, finally bit out the words, "Of course I remember. So what?"

"All you wanted was a chance to be with your dad. And you couldn't have it because he'd died. I'm not dead, Sara. I want to do those things with my son. Why do you want to deny Liam what you wanted yourself? Give us a chance. Come with me, both of you."

CHAPTER EIGHT

IT WAS no time to be having second thoughts.

The plane was just landing. Liam, who had slept for a good chunk of the flight over the pond, was now wide awake, peering out the window, asking questions a mile a minute. Sara was answering them with less than her customary briskness. She didn't look as if she'd slept much at all.

Flynn knew she'd tried because he had never shut his eyes. He'd sat there the whole flight, trying to imagine what was going through her head, what she thought of his heavy-handed emotional manipulation that had got her to agree to come to Ireland, what she was going to think of Dunmorey—what was going to happen next.

He would have preferred to play it cool, to go back to Montana and let her come to the gradual realization that she and Liam belonged with him.

He knew from years of working with reluctant, nervous, highly volatile people that the best results occurred when they thought the story he was doing was their own idea; when they thought it was in their best interest to give him what he wanted; when they trusted him.

He'd given Sara little reason to trust him over the years.

Now she had even less.

But he couldn't leave them behind, couldn't just walk away from what they'd begun to find in Elmer. He loved them. Both of them. Liam as his son, of course. But Sara—Sara was his heart. He couldn't live without her.

He'd thought he had a fair chance of convincing her in Montana. Now he felt like he was starting all over again—from the worst vantage point possible.

Oh, he had no doubt Liam would be delighted. Getting to visit the ancestral castle was draw enough for any little boy, especially one as predisposed to be thrilled as Liam was.

But there was little about Dunmorey to enchant a reluctant woman at the best of times. These were hardly the best. The place was downtrodden and damp.

And, of course, as usual, it was raining.

"Doesn't it ever stop?" he growled into his mobile phone at Dev while they were waiting to board a short commuter flight to Cork. Liam had Sara by the hand and had dragged her over to look out the window at all the planes. He was chattering eagerly as usual. Sara still was barely saying a word.

Flynn didn't like it. He wanted back the passionate devoted Sara of old or the occasionally prickly but generally expansive and good-natured Sara he'd got used to in Elmer. The one who had kissed him so passionately in the kitchen the afternoon he'd ended up leaving wouldn't have been bad either. Or even the slightly remote one of later that evening.

But this one? This one was so quiet she scared him.

It was making him crazy.

But there was damn all he could do about it now.

And he feared that with the rain bucketing down, when she saw Dunmorey things were just going to get worse.

"Clean up around the place as best you can," he told Dev. "I'm bringing company."

"Company? Now?" Dev wasn't pleased. "We aren't exactly in shape for entertaining, if you know what I mean. Ma's not here. I'm up to my eyeballs in horse stuff. And you're going to be, too. Who the hell is this company?"

He hadn't said. Hadn't ever told Dev about Sara—or even about Liam.

Announcing he had a five-year-old son was not something he had wanted to do over the phone. And Dev had been in Dubai when he'd left. He'd just sent his brother an e-mail saying he was heading for the States. Dev knew his book was coming out there soon. And if that was what he thought Flynn had gone to deal with, so be it.

There would be plenty of time to reveal his son's existence, he'd assured himself, once he'd met the boy.

But meeting Sara again had made him put all discussion of his son and the boy's mother on hold. He knew he couldn't talk to his brother about Liam without mentioning his mother. And things had been too tenuous with Sara.

He didn't want to talk about either until he had them both where he wanted them—in his life forever.

At least, that had been the plan before Dev's phone call three days ago.

Now all bets were off.

"Not company, really," Flynn said now. "My son."

There was a dead silence on the other end of the line. Then Dev said, "Bad connection, this. What did you really say? I thought you said your son."

"I did."

"Son?" Dev repeated, stunned.

"That's right. He's five. His name is Liam. He looks…like Will." Flynn started out fine, finished badly. But it was all he could manage.

"Like Will?" Dev was incredulous now.

"You'll see."

"But who is he? When—?"

"I'll explain later. He and his mother are with me. So straighten things up. Put on a clean shirt. Pick up the buckets. We can't do much about the rest of it, but I don't want them tripping over buckets first thing they step inside the door."

Dev made a noise that sounded like a dazed half laugh. "Whatever you say, my lord."

"Stuff it," Flynn said and hung up. Then he mustered up his "everything's under control" face and prayed that it was.

"They're callin' our flight, Dad!" Liam broke away from his mother and came running towards him. "We're almost there!"

And Flynn, catching him up in his arms before Liam could plow into his leg and knock him right over, hoped everything went as smoothly as Liam seemed to believe it would.

"Sorry about the rain," he said to Sara with an apologetic shrug. "It's Ireland."

"No problem. Better for my skin than Montana's wind and cold." Very contained. Very polite. She'd worked on someone's taxes all the way over. But at least she wasn't fighting with him. He hoped that was good.

"We're off to see the castle!" Liam sang out, causing passengers to turn and look, then smile in their direction.

Sara's cheeks reddened as she shushed him.

"He's excited," Flynn said. And as they boarded the plane he knew he was, too.

Personally he'd never been much for fairy tales and castles growing up. The castle part had been all too real, but the fairy-tale endings simply weren't. His father had often seemed more ogre than lord of the realm. And happiness had always been in short supply.

But he'd known happiness—or come close—with Sara and Liam the weeks before the book tour.

And now? Well, he'd asked for this. He'd insisted upon it.

And now they were here. "Be careful what you wish for," his mother had always said. "Take it easy. Take it slow. Be cautious. Be smart."

But he'd jumped in. Apparently he hadn't learned as much patience as he'd thought.

It wasn't your average fairy-tale castle.

It was so much better. So much more...real.

Not that Sara wanted to fall in love with Dunmorey, mind you. It was the last thing she wanted—to get emotionally engaged to a place she was determined to resist.

But how could she resist this?

She hadn't known what to expect. But she'd certainly never expected it to sit on the rise of the hill, dark-gray granite, square and boxy, hunkered down like a petrified stone frog, squatting and scowling as the rain coursed down its face.

A petrified stone frog with a turret that stuck up like an off-center top hat, giving it a slightly rakish, not-quite-put-together air to go with what looked like long-standing endurance. It also looked a little ragged around the edges.

Sara loved it on sight. But at the same time, she began to understand some of the reasons for multitude of phone calls Flynn had dealt with. Being lord of Dunmorey might not be all house parties and riding to the hounds. The sheer weight of it looked as if it could oppress all but the most determined and driven of men. And the farm they'd passed and the stretch of river they'd crossed and the houses they saw were all part of the estate holdings.

All of them were his responsibilities.

"It does, too, have a moat!" Liam exclaimed, craning his neck, pointing at the water they crossed going over the cattle guard onto Dunmorey land. "You said it didn't!" he accused his father.

"Is that what it is?" Flynn looked surprised. "I always thought it was a drainage ditch."

His wry tone made Sara smile. "Perhaps it's all in the mind of the beholder."

He shot her a look of surprise.

"It's beautiful," she said, and meant it. The green rolling hills, the hedges and fences and huge arching trees—it was so lush and green and alive. Montana was just coming into the early days of spring—still spare and often icy.

"You think?" He sounded doubtful. He'd grown quieter and edgier since they'd landed in Cork, she noticed. And the closer they'd got to Dunmorey, the less he'd said.

Was he regretting that he'd brought them?

Certainly he had reason to. Liam was a lovely little boy, and she didn't think so just because he was her son. But he was also a ball of energy, a demand on one's time, a perennial distraction. From the snatches of the phone calls she'd heard between him and his brother over the past two days, Flynn didn't sound as if he needed any distraction.

Of course that was probably why she was here—to keep Liam in check. If she weren't, he'd have to find a nanny.

No, that wasn't fair. He'd made it clear that this invitation wasn't just for Liam. He'd been at pains to be sure she knew he wanted her here, too.

"Besides," he'd added grimly, cracking his knuckles, "you have to see it sometime." Whatever he meant by that.

So she'd come. She'd agreed to his emotional manipulation. But only partly because what he said was true and she knew she didn't have the right to deprive Liam of his father's love just to protect herself.

There was no protection. She came because she wanted to know more about the man whom, against her will, her wish and her better judgment, she loved.

She dared—in her bravest moments—to believe there was something real and honest and true between them. Something that went beyond the physical desire that he relished and even she could no longer deny.

But she wasn't sure. She didn't know.

Coming here she hoped to find out—to learn who Flynn Murray really was beyond the man she knew in Elmer, beyond the charmer she'd long ago fallen in love with.

"I'd like to say it's not as bad as it looks," he said now, jerking her back to the moment at hand as he drove up the lane toward the castle. "But that wouldn't be true. The inside is worse than the outside. The upside, however, is, I might not have it much longer."

His tone was light, but there was a painful undercurrent in his tone that made her look at him sharply.

Sara frowned. "Not have it? Why not?" she asked as he rounded the last curve of the gravel drive and parked by the massive double front doors.

Liam had his seat belt off and the door open almost as soon as the car stopped. He got out and stared straight up at the massive structure that loomed above him. His jaw dropped. "Wow," he said. "Oh, wow."

And then he was off running, trying to see it all. The rain was coming down in earnest. He was getting drenched.

"We can take him in," Flynn said.

But Sara shook her head. "Let him run. He's been in cars and planes too long. He'll dry."

"Don't count on it," Flynn muttered.

"What?"

He just shook his head wryly. "Nothing." He got out, and Sara followed suit, meeting him at the trunk of the car while he got out the luggage. "Why might you not have the castle much longer?"

"The long story or the short one?" Flynn began hauling out their bags. "I could give you a long complicated answer to do with revenues and farm prices and restoration costs. But the short one is, frankly, it can't support itself. Hasn't for a lot of years. It's been cut back, cut back, cut back. Try to reinvest where it will make the most sense and turn the best profit. But it's not entailed any longer. The old man and my grandfather saw to that. They wanted to be able to sell it off if worse came to worst."

"But it's been in your family for three hundred years!"

"And I could be the one to lose it." His jaw tightened and he kneaded the muscles at the back of his neck. "I didn't say I liked the thought," he said gruffly, "but the farm can only do what the farm can do. And the stud is costing plenty of money to get up and going. It will work in the long run. I believe that. But by then I might already have had to sell. It's like trying to keep alive some extinct dinosaur."

"A giant frog," Sara murmured.

Flynn blinked. "What?"

"Never mind." She shouldn't have said a word. "I just…" She shook her head. "I'd hate to see you have to do that."

"So would I," Flynn said fiercely.

She glanced over to where Liam was already trying to scale one of the rough granite walls. "It's a great place for children."

"The gardens are," Flynn agreed. "It's when you're grown-up that it gives you problems."

"I can see where it might," Sara agreed. "But it has definite charm."

Flynn snorted. "Charm? Hardly. Wait'll you see it."

It sounded more like a threat than a promise. But before Sara could reply to that, the door to the house opened and a reasonable facsimile of Flynn came out, grinning.

"Dev," Flynn said. "My younger brother. Dev, this is Sara. She's, um—" he hesitated "—Liam's mother." He jerked his head towards the little boy halfway down the lane.

Dev looked, did a double take. "He is like Will."

Flynn nodded. "Wait'll you meet him."

But Dev was already looking again at Sara. "Liam has a very beautiful mother." His grin widened and he gave her an appreciative look. Then he shook Sara's hand and, by virtue of not letting go, drew her into the entry hall, leaving Flynn to shut the car doors and, glaring at him, carry in the bags.

"It's...nice to meet you," Sara began, then stopped. She'd come through the first entry with its mundane collection of boots and croquet mallets, bows and arrows, walking sticks and umbrellas. It could have been anybody's mud room, albeit bigger and a bit more grand.

But then he steered her through the next set of doors into an entry parlor with gilt and tapestries, marble pillars and a mirror the size of a small lake. She could only stare—at everything else and at her small, insignificant damp bedraggled self.

Dev saw the direction of her gaze. "Huge, isn't it? They put it there to make the room look bigger."

Bigger? It was the size of half her house.

"I should take off my shoes."

"Nah, don't. Your feet will get wet."

She paused, halfway to bending down to take them off. "What?"

"Roof leaks. Not here," Dev said, "but all over upstairs. In the kitchens. Windows let the rain in, too. Carpets are soggy. Floors gets wet. Keep your shoes on," he advised.

"Oh. Right. I, um, will."

"This way," he said and started to lead her past doors that dwarfed her. "I've got a fire in the blue parlor."

As opposed to the red one? she thought a little desperately, a little wildy as she followed him. For if Dunmorey Castle had looked like a squat granite frog from the outside, it was clearly beyond elegant within.

Shabbily elegant, yes. Possibly threadbare in spots. But definitely formal, imposing and historic. As Dev led her to the blue parlor, portraits of men and women with decidedly Murray features stared down their noses at her from both sides of the hallway. They looked austere and remote and judgmental.

A part of her wanted to turn tail and run.

"I'm seeing why Flynn spent so much time in America." Dev pulled open a heavy oak door, and held it for her.

"Yes, the book tour was long and—" Sara began.

"And he had a couple of other things to keep him occupied," Dev finished smoothly. He was smiling, but Sara felt guilty, understanding that she and Liam were those other things.

"I know you needed him here—"

"He's the earl," Dev said simply. "But he is entitled to a life."

"I guess," Sara said. She looked around the blue parlor. The walls were blue, the furniture was leather and oak and on the wall there were more silk tapestries.

"Sit down." Dev gestured to one of the chairs. "I'll yell for Daisy to rustle up some tea."

She didn't imagine he meant literally, but he went out into the hall and bellowed down it.

A young woman's voice bellowed back, "Get it yourself!"

Dev laughed. "That's Daisy. Our right-hand girl. She cooks and cleans, keeps us out of mischief, and apparently thinks she's busy. Probably getting your rooms ready," he reflected.

Sara felt more of an imposition than ever. "She doesn't need—"

"It's her job," Dev said. "She doesn't mind. And she does way more than we have a right to expect. So I'll make the tea. You can stay here or come down to the kitchen with me."

"I…I should help Flynn. Or get Liam," she said, wishing she could do something to help.

"Flynn's fine. And he'll watch your boy. He does look like our Will." He shook his head. "Coming? Hope you don't mind dogs," he said, leading her out into the hallway once more to be surrounded by a pack of three young spaniels and the most enormous Irish wolfhound Sara had ever seen. "Out of the way, you lot." Dev pushed past them. "Go bother Daisy."

With the dog entourage milling around them, Sara followed him down yet another long hallway, trying to keep up and take it all in at the same time.

This hallway was less formal. The formal portraits had given way to paintings and photos of rural landscapes, mounted stags' heads and stuffed salmon. At the far end it got positively mundane with a rack for fishing gear and hooks for dog leashes.

"Here we are," Dev said and led her into a kitchen about the size of her entire downstairs.

You could have roasted an ox in the fireplace at one end of it. And probably once upon a time, people had. Now an Aga was tucked into the opening and actually looked small. A large modern stainless-steel refrigerator hummed alongside it. On the other side she saw a microwave on the countertop.

The sink had both taps and a pump handle. Dev was using the former now, filling the kettle. On the other side of the sink the countertop contained a series of dog dishes, a bright blue baby bath and, beside it, a plastic high chair.

Sara took it all in, but her gaze stopped on the baby bath and the high chair which were even more out of place than the microwave.

Dev plugged in the kettle, then followed her gaze. "Those are Eamon's," he said. "He belongs to Daisy."

"I see. I feel terrible, putting you out this way. Obviously you weren't expecting us."

"Didn't even know about you."

She stared. "Didn't...know?"

He'd been gone almost two months. He'd known about Liam all that time. And he hadn't ever said?

"Sorry. Shouldn't have said that," Dev apologized. "None of our business really. It's what I said, Flynn's entitled to his life. It's just...surprising. I was gone when he left. In Dubai getting our stud. Got an e-mail. He only said business in the States. I had no idea. But it's grand news," he added cheerfully and gave her a long appreciative once-over that would have made her blush if she weren't so confused.

"You didn't even know about Liam?"

"Not till he rang this morning."

Sara didn't know what to think about that.

But Dev had an opinion. "He's always gone his own way, done his own thing, our Flynn. It's what's made this so difficult, him having to take over. Ma reckons he needs a wife to show him the way things ought to be done."

"Really?" Sara said faintly.

"But I'm thinking you're the best thing that's happened to him since...forever, I'd say."

Sara flushed. "That's ridiculous. You don't know me."

"I know Flynn. He isn't known for sharing what's nearest and dearest to him. But if he brought you back here, you matter. And I like the look of him. And he sounds better than he has in ages."

Did he? How had he sounded before? And why?

A hundred inappropriate questions begged to be asked. But as "our Flynn's" footsteps were fast approaching with Liam in tow—she could hear the constant barrage of questions—she didn't ask.

"I saw a fish, Ma!" Liam informed her. "A big fish! And a gee-normous dog!" His eyes were wide, his arms stretched out as far as he could reach. "Did you see him? His name is O'Mally. He's just a puppy, seven months old. Dad said he can sleep with me!"

"He did, did he?"

Flynn shrugged. "Why not? He sleeps with Sid."

"There's only the matter of about a hundred pounds difference."

"I just thought he'd make Liam good company. Make him feel at home."

He was probably right. They'd had a dog, Flash, when Liam was born. But Flash had died last year. She'd told Liam they would get another dog before Sid forgot what it was like to have to share his house. They just needed to find the right one to fill the hole in their lives.

O'Mally looked as if he'd fill almost any hole imaginable.

"Cool, huh?" Liam said. "An' did you see the buckets?"

"Buckets?"

"Upstairs. We took the bags up an' I met Daisy an' her baby an' Dad says there are lots of buckets for the rain."

"We're getting a new roof." Flynn was looking more and more uncomfortable as the revelations continued. Dev, however, was grinning all over his face. He poured the tea into mugs, added milk and passed them around, then added a plate of biscuits—"Cookies," Flynn explained to Liam who looked worried until he saw them—then said, "So tell me where you come from."

Sara let Flynn tell Dev what he wanted him to know. And, of course, Liam chipped in. She didn't say much at all. She just looked around, let the conversation wash over her. As much as she'd liked Dunmorey on sight, she was still having trouble thinking of Flynn as master of it all.

It was huge, magisterial, daunting. The kitchen—despite its great size—was the only place she really felt at home. Probably, she thought stifling a yawn, it was because the kitchen was where she belonged—with the staff.

"You need some rest," Flynn said abruptly. "Let me show you your room. You can take a nap."

"Not me!" Liam protested. "I don't want a nap!"

"By heaven, no. Not you," Dev laughed. "I'll take Mr. Energy with me to the stables."

Liam's eyes got rounder. "You got horses, too?"

"We have a couple. One of them is a brand-new stallion. Come see," Dev invited, then turned to Sara. "I'll keep an eye on him."

Liam hopped from one foot to the other. "Can O'Mally come, too?"

"Liam," Sara admonished.

But Dev just laughed. "Can ducks swim?"

"Yes! C'mon, O'Mally!" And Liam looped his arm high over the dog's back—they were pretty much the same height, Sara noticed—and they trooped out the door after Dev.

In the quiet after their departure, Sara realized that for the first time since Flynn had come back, they were alone.

Flynn seemed to realize it, too, and for once was absolutely silent.

"It's…lovely," Sara said at last. She stopped before she said it was also immense and overwhelming.

"Not lovely," Flynn replied, cracking his knuckles. Then he dipped his hands in his pockets and began to pace. "It's a disaster, in fact. You can see how much needs to be done." He gave a sweep of his hand that seemed to encompass the entire castle.

"Probably should just torch the whole thing," he said bitterly, "but it's so wet, I doubt it would burn!"

"And you don't want it to burn." Sara knew that instinctively.

He hunched his shoulders, then opened the door and gestured for her to follow. "No, I don't want it to burn," he said leading her back down the hall. "And I'd like to show you around more now, but I need to get together the stuff we have to take to the bank tomorrow. So I'll show you to your room so you can rest."

The spaniels followed in their wake. Sara patted their heads and tried to keep up, still gawking. "If there's anything I can do to help—"

Flynn shook his head. "Thank you, but this is our problem. My problem," he corrected himself. He stopped at the foot of the stairs and turned to the spaniels. "No," he said to them in his lord-of-the-manor voice. It was the same voice he'd used to decline her offer of help.

He tried to imagine what the place looked like through her eyes.

The prospect made him wince. All those dour old ancestors with their beady green eyes glaring down at her. Faded rugs. Peeling paint. The dogs milling around. The buckets everywhere.

He was used to it and he still found it appalling. Not the trappings. He could care less about the trappings. But the castle seemed so damn soulless. Not exactly home sweet home.

No, when he thought of home—of warmth and comfort and welcome—he thought of Sara's.

He saw her to her room. Fortunately one with only two buckets—and those empty at the moment. There was a fire in the fireplace, too, warming its usual cold-as-cockles air. Bless you, Daisy, he thought, sending her a silent thank-you.

Sara stood in the middle of the room, looking around in silence, unmoving.

"It's…not exactly what you're used to," he said awkwardly. No warmth. No heart.

Sara turned. "Well, I'll do my best not to muss it up or break anything."

"No," he said quickly, "that's not what I meant. It's just…" But somehow he couldn't express how inadequate it felt—he felt! "I hope you'll be very comfortable here," he said finally. "I'll… see you later."

She nodded. "Thank you."

He turned to go when she said his name. "Flynn?"

Hopefully, he turned back. "Yes?"

"You look tired, too. You should try to get a nap, too." Her face was suddenly flushed and she looked as awkward as he felt.

He sighed wearily. "Nice idea. No time."

Nothing on earth sounded better. He would have loved a nap. With Sara in his arms.

But he couldn't even let himself think about it. He had to come up with a reasonable plan—on paper at least—for Dunmorey's financial future. He shut himself in his study and set to work.

Two hours later he stared bleakly out the window at the coursing rain and faced the fact that he was wasting his time. All his hopes and dreams were clearly fantasies.

Back in the autumn, the plan for the stud had seemed reasonable. Back in February, when he'd left for Elmer, he'd believed in the possibility that they could do this—could have the stud and Dunmorey, too, and it wasn't simply a pipe dream.

And once he'd met Sara again, he'd even dared dream that he could marry her and live happily ever after.

Today in his dripping, crumbling pile of stone, he had no choice but to stare reality in the face. It was going to be one or the other—the castle or the stud. And the future was not in a five-hundred-year-old pile of damp rocks. They would have to sell Dunmorey.

Eight earls before him had done the job. He would be the earl who bit the dust.

And Sara? Well, for all that she said polite things, she looked appalled most of the time. Coercing her into coming with him had been a mistake.

It had seemed like a good idea at the time. Of course he hadn't seen her in a month, and he'd have done anything—said anything—to guarantee that he didn't have to leave her behind again.

But now, despite Liam's enthusiasm for the castle, the stables, even the drainage ditch, for God's sake, and despite Sara's own polite tolerance so far, he knew he'd jumped the gun.

He might be able to impress a five-year-old with the family castle, but Sara was, above all, a realist. She would see Dunmorey for what it was—a mouldering pile of stones that echoed the past and had nothing to offer the future.

As a CPA, she would see the way the bank saw, even if he and Dev had tried to pretend otherwise. They'd been blinded by having grown up here. They saw it no more clearly than Liam did.

Pity little boys didn't run banks, he thought grimly.

Even their mother seemed to have seen it more clearly than they had, perhaps because she'd only married into the disastrous mess.

After his father's death, the duchess had told Flynn time and again that if he wanted to keep Dunmorey he'd have to marry money.

"It's what your father did," she'd reminded him bluntly. His mother, too, was a realist. She'd even laughed and promised to bring him home a rich wife when she'd left to visit her sister in Australia after Christmas.

"Yeah," Flynn had said, "you do that."

But he didn't need her to find him a wife. He'd already found the wife he wanted—Sara.

He didn't want anyone but Sara.

And now he'd invited her to watch him fail.

Sara saw a note had been shoved under her door when she got up.

When she'd opened her eyes to the amazing four-poster bed and the heavy dark ornate bureau and chairs beside the fireplace, she had for an instant thought she was still asleep, caught in some very vivid dream.

And then she realized where she was. She scrambled out of bed, switched on a light, then riffled through her suitcase for a pair of jeans and a sweater. She pulled them on quickly because the fire had gone out and the room was cold.

Exhausted, a little bit dazed and a lot uncertain, she had taken refuge in slumber. And for once her body had cooperated, and she'd fallen asleep the instant her head had hit the pillow.

And now it was—she glanced at her watch—nearly 6 p.m.? Good grief! And she had left Liam in Dev's care all afternoon.

She stuffed her feet into her shoes, then picked up the note.

In Flynn's spiky handwriting, she read, "Liam's asleep in the room next to yours. I've left a light on and a string trail downstairs for when he wakes. Check on him if you want."

She felt a bit less guilty, breathed a little easier then. She took time to wash her face, comb her hair, then straighten the covers on the amazing, opulent four-poster bed. Then she opened the door and tried to decide which of the rooms on either side of hers was Liam's. The line of string leading from under one of the doors was the clue.

She eased open the door. There was a low light on in the room, making it easy for her to see Liam all but buried beneath a thick duvet in the midst of a gigantic bed.

Beside him, four times as big, lay O'Mally. He opened one eye and watched Sara approach. She hoped he was as friendly when he was sleeping with Liam as he had been earlier. Apparently he decided she was safe because he thumped his tail twice, then laid his head back down and closed his eyes even as Sara approached the bed.

Liam was sprawled on his stomach, very little of him visible beyond his face, his tousled hair and part of one arm, which was crooked around Curious George. His back was snug against O'Mally's. Clearly they were a pair.

Sara smiled, then leaned over and pressed a light kiss to Liam's temple. His lips moved in a smile. His father's smile. His father's mouth. The mouth, she now knew, that had belonged to generations of his Murray forebears, not to mention his uncle Dev. For him she was glad they had come.

For herself…well, it was certainly an experience.

She settled the duvet around him more closely, then scratched O'Mally behind the ear and was rewarded with another tail thump on the bed. Fearing that it would wake Liam, she turned to leave. Taped on the inside door handle she saw another note: "Liam, follow the string and find me. Love, Dad."

At least there was no doubt that Flynn loved his son. She was happy for Liam.

She didn't have to follow the string.

When she finally came downstairs after stopping to look her fill this time at the portrait in the hall and down the stairwell, the sound of raised voices arguing in one of the rooms drew her.

She heard the words: "Dunmorey" and "sell" and "don't add up." That was Flynn. Then she heard Dev's more Irish inflections arguing about paddocks and stalls and future earnings.

And then she heard Flynn roar, "There won't be any earnings unless we sell, damn it! That's what I'm trying to tell you!"

The voices lowered again, but Sara hurried away, not wanting to eavesdrop, much less walk in on a family quarrel.

She hurried down the hallway past the disapproving ancestors and ducked into what turned out to be the formal dining room. Her mother's dining room table was big. But it didn't come close to the size of this one. Her mother didn't have two pairs of three-foot-tall silver candelabras on hers. Sara had no trouble imagining them lit and elegant lords and ladies—generations of them—taking meals here.

Because the voices continued, she did, too. She found a billiards room and a room she thought of as the yellow parlor because of its color. She found a music room and a small office that looked, from the delicate feminine furniture, as if it must belong to Flynn's mother, the countess.

She tried to imagine what a countess would be like. She was glad the countess wasn't here. She was quite certain Flynn's mother would not be as approving as Dev was.

Because Sara knew had no business in the countess's office—could you get arrested for it? she wondered—she hurried back out.

There was lots else to see. It was not the sort of house she was normally invited to. Every piece of furniture, every knickknack, every doily and painting doubtless had a memorable history.

She could see where it would be hugely demanding. But at the same time it was a shame no one paid any attention to it—because clearly no one did.

Most of the rooms were dusty and neglected. If just one girl was in charge of the cleaning—Daisy of the baby and the biscuits—if she got to each room once a month, Sara thought she would be doing well.

She was just heading down the hallway towards the kitchen to see if she could make a cup of tea, when she heard Dev's voice.

"Be damned if I'm askin' you to sell!" A door banged furiously down the hall.

Quickly Sara ducked into the kitchen and was putting on the kettle when Dev shoved open the door and stopped in surprise at the sight of her.

"Ah, and you're awake, then." He was breathing hard and made a conscious effort to slow himself down. "Did we wake you, yellin' like that?"

"No. I—were you yelling?"

He grinned. "Tactful of you."

Sara smiled. "Would you like some tea?"

"I would. Or something a damn sight stronger. He's a pain in the arse, your man."

"Not mine," Sara said quickly.

But Dev didn't seem to notice. "As if I'd expect him to sell the damn castle to fund the stables!"

"Is he?" She knew he'd mentioned it, but couldn't believe he'd decided so quickly.

"Trying not to. It will kill him to have to do it. There has to be another way!" Dev looked like he wanted to kick something.

"He's not doing it lightly," she said. "I'm sure."

"Hell, no, he's not doing it lightly. He's got a streak of responsibility as wide as the feckin' Nile, does our Flynn. Blatting on about 'the future!' But it will gut him to do it on account of the old man."

"Old man?"

"Our dearly departed father," Dev said bitterly. There was apparently no love lost between the old earl and his youngest son, either. "Never gave Flynn the respect he deserved. Blamed him for Will dying."

Sara gasped.

Dev gritted his teeth. "Like he'd got shot and come home on purpose just for that." He stalked across the room and stood with his hands braced on the kitchen sink, staring blindly out into the darkness. "The old man should've blamed Will, damn it. Stupid helpful bugger, always trying to do the right thing," he said in a choked voice.

Flynn had called Will a saint. But she had no idea what happened. He hadn't told her that.

Dev did. Then, "Left Flynn holding the bag. And the old man telling him he was useless, that he was never going to measure up."

"How could he possibly think that?" Sara was outraged. She couldn't imagine any father believing, much less saying such a thing.

Dev shrugged. "It's the way he was. Now Flynn's earl, he's doing his best to prove the old bugger wrong. I figured I could help if we got the stud going. It would help. I just didn't think it would cost this much."

"How much?"

He told her. It was a substantial sum.

"Only way he thinks we can do it is to sell," Dev said glumly.

Sara made the tea, though she thought something stronger might definitely be in order. Since she didn't know where the whiskey was, she filled three mugs.

"Brave soul you are, if you're going to take it to him." Dev raised his brows. "Of course he might not act like such an eejit around you."

Sara hoped that was true. But even if he did, she understood more now. Appreciated the pressures on Flynn—from within and without. She admired the amount of time he'd spent with them in Elmer. The flurries of phone calls made a lot more sense.

She carried the tray down the hall and tapped on the door where she'd heard them arguing earlier. For a long moment there wasn't any reply, and she thought he might have left.

But then she heard a chair squeak and Flynn's gruff voice. "Scared to come back in?"

Balancing the tray with one hand, she opened the door. "No. I just brought you some tea."

He leapt out of his chair and raked a hand through his hair. It looked as if he'd done that already a time or two. Quickly he crossed the room to take the tray from her. "I thought you were Dev. Sorry."

Sara shut the door and followed him back across the room. "I'm glad I'm not."

Flynn grimaced. "You heard?"

"Some. Not all of it. When I came downstairs you were, um, talking. So I went along the hall. I was making a cup of tea when Dev came in. He's upset."

"Why? He's getting what he wants!"

"But he thinks it's coming at too great a cost."

"He told you?" Flynn scowled furiously.

"He's worried about you."

Flynn snorted. "Doesn't need to be. I'll survive. *Eireoidh Linn.* It's the bloody family motto!" He prowled the room with exactly the same ferocity that Dev had displayed in the kitchen.

Sara watched him, then sat down on one of the chairs by the fire. "Yes, but it doesn't sound as if he wants it at the expense of Dunmorey."

"Well, how the hell else is he going to get his horses? They're a potential moneymaker. The castle isn't! It's—"

"A potential moneymaker, too."

He stared at her. "What?"

"I said, the castle certainly can earn you some money."

Flynn gave a disbelieving laugh. "Yeah, right. Did you trip over a bucket and hit your head? It's a money pit, not the other way around! And the new roof—which I promise you it will be getting sooner rather than later—is only one of its problems."

"But it has so many possibilities, too!"

"Try telling the bank that."

"If you want me to, I will."

Their gazes met, locked. She knew she'd overstepped, put her foot in family business where it had no business being. But what she said was absolutely true.

Flynn just stared at her a long moment, then raked his hand through his hair again. "Look, Sara, I know you mean well. You're kind to be thinking anything good about this place. But even my father, who lived and breathed Dunmorey, knew it was just a matter of time until we'd have to let it go."

"Then your father was exceedingly shortsighted."

Flynn's brows arched in surprise. And from the look on his face, Sara wondered if anyone had ever dared dispute the old earl's wisdom regarding the ancestral pile. Or anything else for that matter.

Taking advantage of his look of astonishment, she pressed on. "You're so used to it that you don't see what you've got here."

"On the contrary, I know exactly what we've got here. We've got a pile of rubble and mildew, going from bad to worse."

"Only if you give up on it." She jumped up, needing to move, as well. "You have this amazing history. Hundreds of years of it. I've heard you tell Liam bits of it. And this gorgeous place—no, truly, it is gorgeous." She forestalled his protest. "The woods, the meadows...the moat—" she grinned "—and the castle, too. It's just run-down. But it must have seen bad times now and then. Every place does. But truly, Flynn, it's magical. Didn't Liam think it was magical? It just needs work, care. Love."

"Money," Flynn stuck in.

"Well, who's making the bestseller lists these days?"

"Banks aren't impressed by bestseller lists."

"Have you asked them?"

"I wasn't on it when I last talked to the bank. But—"

"Then you don't know. They'll think you're a hot commodity now. And if you refurbished some of the rooms, you could turn them into a conference or retreat center. You have this huge amazing dining room—" she stopped, embarrassed "—I snooped while you and Dev were…discussing. But truly, it would be great for meetings, for banquets. Have you ever tried any of that?"

"My father would have died first."

"Well, your father has died first. Now it's your turn." She warmed to her topic even as he raised his brows. "You could make part of it a bed-and-breakfast. Think how many people would love to have tea and kippers with the lord of the manor!"

Flynn groaned. "Sara, we don't eat kippers."

Sara ignored him. She was on a roll. "Corned beef and cabbage then. Whatever. When you get the stud going, you can have guests who come to see the horses. You can do history weekends and have experts talk to people who come to learn about life on the manor. There are tons of possibilities. This castle is your greatest resource, Flynn. You can't sell it!"

"I can't afford it."

Sara flopped back down in her chair again and stared up at him. "Or," she said airily, "I guess you could just give up."

"Damn it, Sara!" His jaw tightened.

She shrugged lightly. "Do whatever you want. Liam's seen it now. We could go home tomorrow."

Their gazes clashed again—hers challenging, his a hard furious glare. The silence went on…and on.

She knew he was fighting himself even more than he was fighting her.

"You used to be a sweet young thing," Flynn said gruffly when he'd unclenched his jaw enough to get the words out. "What the hell happened?"

Sara smiled. "I met you. I had Liam. I grew up."

CHAPTER NINE

"So what do you suggest?" Flynn leaned against the bookcase, hoping he looked calmer and more in control than he felt.

It was bad enough to finally come to the realization that he was going to have to sell to support the start-up of the stud, and then have Dev yell and carry on and storm out the door like he'd been insulted.

It was beyond infuriating to have Sara in here now, taking his brother's part.

Most of all, he didn't understand why she was coming up with all these ideas out of nowhere. She didn't even like the place!

"I suggest you don't do anything drastic, like even thinking about selling Dunmorey, until you've tried some of the things I've told you."

"And I'm going to do this how?" he demanded impatiently. "I know you're trying to help, Sara. But I've told you, we're going to the bank tomorrow. If we want anything from them, we have to show them a new business plan illustrating how we intend to maximize our assets."

"So do that. Show them plans for a retreat center, guest accommodations, manor house tours, the whole kit and kaboodle."

It was tempting. God, it was tempting.

So was she. Sara in a fit of enthusiasm was a sight to behold, her cheeks flushed, her eyes bright, her whole body quivering.

He saw the same drive in her now that he'd seen six years ago when she'd been focused on med school.

And in spite of himself, he felt her kindle the same enthusiasm in him. But still he hesitated, afraid to hope, to believe.

"Why?" he asked.

"What?" She frowned.

"Why do you care?"

She opened her mouth. Then she hesitated, too, and he thought she might just shrug, blow him off, change the subject. But she didn't.

She looked him straight in the eye. "Because you do."

It was the truth.

She'd been going to give him the truth back in Elmer, the morning he'd ended up in New York. She would have dared to tell him then—but was glad she hadn't after he left her.

But this leaving had not been like the first one. He had called every day. He had come back, and not just for Liam. For her as well.

He'd brought them to Ireland for reasons she wasn't clear on yet. Well, no, that wasn't accurate. The Liam reasons she understood very well. He wanted his son. He loved his son.

And the reasons he'd brought her? Those she desperately hoped she knew. But she couldn't ask. She could only guess.

And because she understood now how much Dunmorey and all that it entailed mattered to him, she would do whatever was necessary to help him save the castle.

"Look," she said when he didn't speak, "I think I can help. I don't just do taxes, I do business plans, as well. Ranchers are always going in for loans. It's the story of their lives. And I've worked with a lot of them. I know ranches aren't castles, but they cost a lot to run. You have to be creative, to think outside the box. I can do that. And I can write it up—if you want."

He didn't answer. He just stared at her.

And Sara knew she had misread everything.

"Or not," she said hastily. "I should keep my mouth shut. Not interfere. It's your castle, your brother. It's none of my business."

But Flynn just shook his head. "I think you just made it your business," he said, never taking his eyes off her. "Dear God, Sara. I hope you're right. Let's get Dev back in here and talk."

They talked most of the night. Sara was in intense mode, tossing out ideas right and left. He would happily have just sat there and watched her, but her enthusiasm was catching. And a surprising number of her ideas tickled his fancy—from the pony rides for children to getting restoration experts to come and teach their skills using Dunmorey as their canvas.

"Like painting workshops," she said. "Only, you'd get a lot of work done that way."

Flynn could see the potential, could feel the energy growing. The only idea he balked at was her suggestion of writers' weeks.

She grinned at him. "They could come and sit at your feet."

"Don't be daft," Flynn said.

But Dev said, "Write it down."

Sometime in the middle of the night, Liam woke up once, followed the string down, O'Mally at his side, and found them in Flynn's study. He blinked at them sleepily. "Whatcha doin'? Why's it dark?"

"Because it's three in the morning, boyo," Dev told him.

Liam wrinkled his nose. "How come I'm hungry?"

"Because you slept through dinner," Sara said. She looked at Flynn. "Can I get him something to eat?"

He stood up. "You stay here and work on this horse stuff with Dev. Liam and I will make tea."

"Tea?" Liam's nose wrinkled again.

"Food," Flynn promised. He took his son's hand and led him towards the door, glancing back to give Sara a nod of encouragement.

Truth be told, he was the one who was encouraged.

Encouraged? Hell, it was all he could do not to dance down the hallway, bad leg and all. Sara was interested! Sara was involved!

Sara didn't hate Dunmorey!

He and Liam made tea and sandwiches and piled biscuits on a plate, then carried it all back down the hallway to his office. Sara and Dev were sitting on the floor. They both looked up when he and Liam came in, and Sara gave him a smile that nearly stopped his heart.

"I think it will work," she said. Her voice had a thread of exhaustion in it, but there was elation, too. "Let me type it up and you can take it in tomorrow. It will certainly give them something else to chew over. I don't think, looking at it, that they will turn you down flat."

Flynn set down the tray and reached down to haul her to her feet. "You don't, huh?"

"No, I—" She started to explain.

But Flynn had all the explanation that he needed. He kissed her.

He'd kissed her in the airport when he'd got back from the tour. But it had been a chaste kiss, a kiss capable of being witnessed by their five-year-old.

He had been all too aware of having nearly scandalized Liam in the kitchen the day he left.

This kiss was spontaneous, not calculated. Spur-of-the-moment like that one had been. But he'd intended it to say thank you, to say how glad he was she'd come, that she was involved, sharing Dunmorey, sharing his life.

He certainly hadn't intended the heat of it to deepen, to catch fire, to become so much more—to want so much more.

Tell his body that!

It was as if the weeks of frustration, of need, of desire had finally taken their toll, as if all the willpower he'd used to bide his time, to court, to woo, to wait, was gone. The dam burst.

The mere taste of Sara's lips made him weak-kneed with longing and hard with desire. It was like touching a match to a pile of dry shavings. Sparks shot. Flames soared. Her lips parted. Their tongues tasted, teased, tangled.

"Please, not in front of the children," Dev said with loud good cheer. Then "Pass me a sandwich," he said to Liam.

Sara jumped back. Flynn flung himself down on the sofa and tried to get a grip. He didn't want a grip. He wanted Sara upstairs in bed naked.

"Have a sandwich," Dev said and passed him one.

"I don't see why you want me to come along."

It wasn't the first time Sara had said this as Flynn took her by the hand and kept a firm grip on it as they walked towards the bank. "I don't belong here."

"You absolutely belong here." Flynn held the door for her. "You wrote the plan."

"But it's your castle. Your future."

"Your plan."

"But it's just speculative at this point."

"So you can tell him that as well. Sit." He pointed her to a chair, then, when she sat, loomed over her making sure she didn't bolt. At least that was what it felt like.

It was insane, dragging her to their business meeting. She didn't know how such things were done in Ireland, she said. She knew more than he did about business plans in any country, he countered. He'd write anything she wanted forever for her if she'd do this for him, he added.

She wondered if he'd write "I love you, Sara," if she asked him to. It was so much the only thing she wanted—had ever wanted from him. But how could she ask that?

She had his kiss. It had been a wonderful kiss. A reminder of the kiss in Elmer. But somehow even better.

More intense? More emotional? More from the heart?

Or was she kidding herself?

"Mr. Monaghan will see you now."

Mr. Monaghan was weedy, slender, with a too-big suit and a too-small moustache. He wore half-glasses that slipped down his nose. He shook hands with them all, but his gaze skated right over Sara.

He was all attentive to Flynn, though, "my lording" him so often it made Sara's teeth hurt. But even while he was doing so, he nattered on about grave concerns, serious doubts and ended by saying, "I really don't think we can offer much help."

His unhappy, yet almost obsequious negativism, made her want to strangle him. She didn't blame Flynn when he shoved her business plan across the desk and said in his Earl's Voice, "Read this."

Mr. Monaghan sat back and blinked, but took the proffered papers and began to read.

They waited in silence. The clock ticked. Outside, cars puttered past on the street. Inside, Dev drummed his fingers on his thigh. Flynn didn't move a muscle or make a sound. Sara held her breath instinctively and had to force herself to breathe.

As he read, Mr. Monaghan's brows lifted a little. And then a little more. And then he cocked his head and pushed his glasses up. Sara glanced at Dev. He was leaning forward a little. Flynn was looking intent.

"Hmm," murmured Mr. Monaghan. Then, "Mmm." He went on more rapidly to the next page and the next.

"What did you have in mind with using the castle as a site of training historical restorationists?" he asked.

Dev and Flynn looked at Sara.

She took a breath and jumped in.

The questions came fast and furious after that. Mr. Monaghan moved back and forth through the business plan asking for clarifications, making notes, nodding, pushing his glasses up, and murmuring, "Yes, I see. Yes, that could do very well. Yes, an interesting notion."

And then set the papers in a neat stack on his desk and sat back and smiled at Flynn for the first time. "Well, my lord, this looks quite promising. I will, of course, have to take it to the board. But I see no impediments now. Let us hope that Dunmorey lives up to its potential. I feel confident it can. I'm sure we'll enjoy doing business together."

In an ancestral sense, Flynn had always known Dunmorey was *home.* But even though he'd grown up loving its grounds and its walls and its stolid granite self, he'd never felt at home there.

Until now.

"It's amazing what a bit of money can do for a place, isn't it?" Dev said three weeks after the loan was approved. And yes, there was a new roof and new paint and new linens and cleaned draperies.

But it wasn't any of those that made the real difference.

The difference was Sara.

It was the vases of fresh flowers she put in every room. It was the music she played. It was the warmth of sunlight—was it his imagination or could Sara actually make the sun come out?—splashing across the warm dark-walnut dining room table.

It was the way she left windows open and doors ajar so that breezes and boys and dogs could wander freely in and out. It was the smell of baking—of breads and biscuits, tarts and cakes—as she and Daisy spurred each other on to greater accomplishments.

It was the miles of wooden railway that she allowed Liam and the boys from the manor farm, Joe and Frank, to run in and through the yellow parlor. It was the bucket of Legos, the Star Wars guys, it was the comfortable way she encouraged Liam and O'Mally to sprawl on the rug while Liam drew pictures.

There was joy in Dunmorey for the first time in Flynn's memory. There was the sound of laughter, of little boys' feet pounding down the hallway.

He didn't remember ever laughing here before Sara came.

He didn't ever remember family meals around the big oak table in the kitchen. He and Dev had eaten there occasionally when it was just the two of them. But now they always ate there—not just he and Dev and Sara and Liam, but often, too, Daisy and little Eamon. One afternoon, to his astonishment, they'd even been joined by Mrs. Upham.

He'd expected Mrs. Upham to criticize Sara's familiarity and had been ready to defend it. But even Mrs. Upham had been charmed.

"Hard worker, that girl," Mrs. Upham said. "Gives her all." It was her highest accolade.

"She does," Flynn agreed.

She had—ever since she'd got here. Had worked almost nonstop on whatever needed to be done. And when she took a break, it wasn't to actually rest, but to turn to doing her Elmer clients' taxes.

He worried that she was working too hard. He wanted to tell her to stop. He wanted to care for her and cosset her and take her to bed and ask her to marry him. But he was afraid to rock the boat.

He'd jumped the gun once before. He'd made her angry, scared her away. So as much as he desperately wanted her in his bed, wanted her to be his forever, he held his peace. He didn't want to scare Sara away.

As wonderful a home as she was turning Dunmorey into, he sensed that she wasn't ready yet.

She still hurried past the stern, formal portraits in the hallway. She only went into the formal dining room to polish the silver. And she stayed away from the rose parlor—the most formal one—where his mother always entertained guests.

"You can do what you like with it," he told her. "Change it if you want."

"No." She shook her head. "Some people prefer that."

"You mean Rawsby's wife?" A few days earlier an old school friend and his new bride had stopped for a visit. Jack had been happy enough to get down on the floor and play with Liam and his trains. But Charlotte, his wife, had sat by primly and looked as if she could hardly wait to escape.

It was only when Sara had suggested they take tea in the rose parlor that Charlotte had deigned to smile. But she hadn't had much to say to Sara even then. Her conversation had been with her husband or Flynn.

"She was rude," he told Sara after. "Don't pay any attention to her."

After all, the rest of the castle and its inhabitants and its tenants responded to Sara's warmth, to her cheer, to her unfailing hard work.

She showed them possibilities that they barely believed existed.

Dev had laughed that first night when she'd suggested giving pony rides to the children of tourists who would be coming to view the house.

But when she pressed the issue, he found some ponies in the neighborhood and offered them board if he could use them for rides. He hired two teenage girls who, when they weren't drooling over Flynn and Dev, actually helped with the children. They were a great success.

"How do you think of these things?" Flynn asked her one night when they went for a walk down by the lake. It was another habit they'd fallen into most evenings. They walked and talked and shared their days.

Sara shrugged. "I just look around and think, What would I like to do? Chances are pretty good if I'd like it, someone else will too."

And it was how Flynn came to build the tree house.

He didn't tell Sara what he was doing. And he swore Liam to secrecy. He didn't know if she would think it was foolish and that he'd be better spending his time on something else, or if she would say he was ruining a fine old tree—which his father had once said when at twelve Flynn had suggested it—or if he would regret having done it once he had.

But as a child he'd wanted a tree house more than anything. He'd wanted a place to go to get away from the castle, from its demands and confines. He'd wanted a place—a home—of his own.

So he took a page out of Sara's book and decided that if he'd once wanted it, maybe someone else would, too. Like Liam.

Or Sara herself.

So every afternoon after he'd worked on estate business, he and Liam disappeared down into the woods. The tree he picked was the tree he'd climbed as a boy. It was the tree that had been his haven even without a house.

It was an ancient ash with low spreading branches that made it perfect for what he had in mind. He brought the lumber down one evening when Sara was busy with a bunch of guests who were being shown around the stables. She and Dev had to be there. He and Liam did not. The timing was perfect.

The work was harder than he'd thought. His leg made climbing difficult. But Liam was as agile as a monkey and as fearless as Flynn had always been.

"Hand it to me, Dad! I can do it, Dad!" He was thrilled with the idea of their secret hideaway. He never stopped grinning.

"What are you up to?" Sara asked him more than once when Liam would giggle.

"Can't tell. Me 'n' Dad got a secret."

And they had a bond—a sense of joy and accomplishment and connection—that he'd never shared with his own father.

But that had been the earl's choice, Flynn realized, not his.

They weren't telling her something.

They went off together every afternoon, Flynn and Liam, and she had no idea where they were or what they were doing.

It made her nervous, edgy. It worried her.

Everything had been going so well with the castle, with the stables, with all their ideas. Sometimes she found it hard to believe what some paint and paper, spit and polish, and a whole lot of elbow grease could accomplish.

She felt good about it. Good about everything.

Almost.

There was something wrong between her and Flynn—and she didn't know what it was.

He loved what they were doing in the castle. She could see it in his body language, in his eyes, in his face. He threw himself into all of it. Worked on his new book in the morning, but in the afternoons he got involved in working on the restoration. Or he had until recently.

Two weeks ago he'd disappeared one afternoon. She hadn't thought anything of it at first. He often had meetings with his tenants or local tradesmen that she knew nothing about.

But then he began to take Liam. They didn't say where they were going. And if she asked, Liam would only say, "Can't tell. It's a secret." And he'd grin.

She didn't imagine it could be too terrible if Liam was grinning about it. But she didn't like him having secrets from her. Didn't like him having secrets with his father. Didn't like being left out.

She felt just a little left out. Because of that—and because after having pushed and cajoled and manipulated her until she'd actually come to Ireland, now he had backed off.

They'd had one passionate inappropriate kiss which she put down to jet lag—and thanked God Dev had interrupted—and that was it. Well, besides some hand holding when they walked down by the lake.

Maybe he was getting cold feet. Maybe seeing her here was making him realize they didn't belong together. It was possible, goodness knew. Every time she walked past that damn mirror in the entry hall she felt small and out of place.

Maybe Flynn felt the same way. Maybe he just didn't know how to tell her.

It was possible.

And it was particularly possible to think so today. Having just endured her first formal tea with a dozen society dames—in the rose parlor no less—she was feeling out of sorts and out of place.

She didn't need to finally get rid of them all and come out into the garden for a breath of fresh air and a bit of equilibrium to spot Flynn and Liam coming up the path from the woods together. They were talking, laughing—and then they saw her and Liam said, "Shhh!"

"We missed you at tea," Sara said, annoyed. Not Liam, of course. But every one of the women had hoped Flynn would drop in. They'd been polite enough to her, but they were obviously a little uncertain about her status. As was she, to be honest. "Mother of the earl's love child" was not exactly a preferred role in their society.

"We were busy," Flynn said. "Down in the woods," he added. He hesitated, looking nervous, wary.

And Sara felt suddenly even more nervous and wary, too.

"In the woods?" She frowned. "Clearing trails?" It was the only sensible thing she could think of that they'd have been doing down there. And even that, given Flynn's leg, didn't seem sensible for him.

"No." Liam grabbed her hand. "C'mon. Come see."

She dug in her heels until she looked at Flynn.

He shrugged. "Why not?"

Liam was pulling her down the path now. She walked this way with Flynn most evenings. "Where are we going?"

"To see what we been doin'."

Still mystified, still a little wary, Sara allowed herself to be towed. It was a warm evening for midspring. The flowers on the garden paths were dancing in the breeze. They turned away from the lake and went deeper into the woods until they reached the far edge overlooking the fields and the river.

Liam stopped abruptly. "There!" He pointed up.

"What?' Sara's gaze followed his finger. "Where?"

At first she didn't see what he was pointing at. But then, about thirty feet up, amid the boughs, she thought she saw sawn planks. Her eyes widened and she turned to look at them. "Is that a tree house?"

Liam bobbed his head. "Me 'n' Dad built it! It's a-mazing! You gotta come see!" He pulled on her hand again until they reached the tree. Then he let go and began scrambling up through the branches. "Follow me."

But before she did, Sara turned to look at Flynn. "This is what you were doing? Building a tree house? The two of you?"

He gave a small nod. "I thought about…what you said…" He looked away, then back at her. "What you said about…if you wanted something, maybe someone else would want it too…."

"You mean, like Liam?"

"Like Liam," he agreed, then met her gaze. "And you."

* * *

And that was how she knew.

Flynn had brought them to Dunmorey for the castle—to show his son his heritage, his history, all those stones piled upon stones. It was impressive. It was, in its way, beautiful. Certainly it was memorable.

But in building the tree house—with his own hands, with his own heart—he had made them a home.

And that was why, after they put Liam to bed that night, she laced her fingers through Flynn's and looked up into his eyes. "I love you," she murmured.

It was a truth she had held in her heart too long.

Now she offered it to him.

She didn't know which of them moved first. Didn't know whether she wrapped her arms around him or if he swept her up into his embrace and bore her away to his bedroom.

It was not a "lord of the manor" room. Even after the recent refurbishment, he had insisted on keeping his own boyhood room and refused to move into the old earl's chambers. Everything was simple, neat, functional.

It was fine with Sara. The trappings didn't matter, only the man.

She didn't want any other man. Never had.

If she belonged with any man, Flynn Murray was the one.

He laid her on his bed and came down beside her. And even fully clothed she could feel the heat of his body next to her. His hands slid under her sweater, stroking her skin. And against her softness, she could feel the calluses on his fingers. Workman's hands, she thought with a smile.

He made his living with words. They were a tool. He used them easily, smoothly, cleverly. But his hands had built the tiny hidden house, the home he'd made for the three of them.

She sought his hands and drew them away from her skin,

touched her lips to them. Kissed his fingers. Nibbled on each in turn. Sucked them.

"Sar'," he murmured. "You are askin' for it."

She smiled. "I know."

Her words seemed to galvanize him. He pushed up to kneel awkwardly on the bed and strip her sweater over her head. She wriggled out of it, then reached up to do the same to him. Then, with his chest bared, she ran her hands over his hair-roughened skin, drew light circles around his nipples, made him catch his breath.

His fingers made quick work of the button and zip of her jeans, then he tugged them down her legs and ran warm, roughened fingers back up them from her instep to the juncture of her thighs.

It was Sara's turn to gasp as he slipped a finger inside the leg opening of her panties and skimmed the part of her that pulsed for his touch. She raised up and fumbled with the fastener of Flynn's jeans. But her fingers trembled and he groaned and said, "Let me."

He had them undone in seconds. But then it was her turn to tug them down over his hips and down to his knees. He shifted awkwardly on his bad leg to let her slip them past, but it was difficult and he cursed.

"No," Sara said, and she gave him a push, toppling him over, then she sat up to pull them off him.

"It's ugly," he said. "You don't want to look."

"It's you," she said. "I want to see every inch of you. Please." She met his gaze then in the half-light. "Please," she repeated.

He sighed and swallowed, then lay back and let her look her fill. Six years ago she'd been too innocent, too circumspect to dare to do what she did tonight. Six years ago she'd been caught up in a fantasy. This was reality. This Flynn was a flesh-and-blood man, not a dream of her youth.

He had wounds and imperfections. So did she. She bent her head and kissed his chest, his hard flat belly, his thighs, the scarred and puckered flesh above his knee. And when she did, her hair brushed lightly against him. Made him tense. Made him quiver. Made him reach for her.

"I want you, Sar'. Now." His voice was ragged, desperate, urgent.

But no more than her need was. And when he reached for her, drew her up against him and rolled her over beneath him, she was all too willing to accommodate, to mould her body to his, to reach between them and take him in.

His breath hissed through his teeth. "Yess. Sar', it's been so long. Too long. Don't ever—never—" He couldn't finish, could only move. And Sara moved with him, filled with him.

It was everything it had been six years ago and more. And this time he took her with him over the edge. And when he groaned her name, she whispered his.

And later when he slept, she kissed his hair, his cheek, his jaw. And smiled through her tears with the joy of believing her youthful dream was even better than a dream.

It was real.

CHAPTER TEN

THE sun in her face woke her.

Sara blinked, feeling fuzzy, warm and boneless. Also momentarily disoriented. And then delighted as she remembered where she was—in Flynn's bed.

If loving Flynn six years ago had been the stuff of dreams, this loving had been far better.

Six years ago they'd spent a night of desperate beauty, stolen from the real world.

But last night had been a night of joy, of tenderness, of passion, the culmination of the sharing of their lives built on weeks—months—of getting to know each other for real.

It had been perfect.

The only thing better would be if he were still here. The pillow where he'd laid his head still bore the indentation. She reached out a hand and stroked the soft cotton and felt it was cool to the touch, so he had been gone awhile.

She didn't remember him leaving. She did remember his kiss. Or had she only dreamed it?

No matter. There would be more.

A lifetime's more.

Of course they would go back to Elmer eventually. Maybe they would marry there? Or here? It didn't matter.

She only needed him.

He'd asked her once in the middle of the night, while they were lying wrapped in each other's arms, what had happened. What was different? Why now?

"Not that I'm not glad," he'd said with a shaky laugh. "I'd just like to know so in case I annoy you, I can do it again."

"The tree house," she'd told him. "You have all this and yet you made that for us. A home."

It could still cause her heart to skip, her eyes to prick, her throat to tighten. And the thought always made her smile.

She didn't suppose they could get married in the tree house. Earls, even unstuffy ones like Flynn, probably drew the line at that.

They'd have to talk about it though. He'd ask her to marry him again. Maybe he'd ask her there.

Or maybe this time she'd ask him. A man didn't have to do all the asking. He'd done it once. Maybe this time it was her turn.

If he were here now, she'd ask him. Where was he?

She rolled over and checked the clock. Ten o'clock? Good heavens!

Instantly she leapt out of bed, dragged on yesterday's clothes and dashed to her own room, hoping Liam wouldn't see her.

But no one saw her. Everyone else had doubtless arisen long ago. She supposed Flynn had made Liam breakfast already. She pulled a brush through her hair. It was in one of its uncooperative moods. She should have taken time for a shower, but she'd need a shower later.

This morning, she had told Flynn yesterday, she and Liam were going to clean out the old chicken house.

"Fresh organic eggs for our guests," she'd said.

And he'd shaken his head. "More projects."

"Yes."

Besides, it was fun to do some hard physical labor, especially when you could see how much better things looked when you were done. So she'd need a shower after the chicken house when she and her clothes would be far grubbier.

She stuffed her feet into her shoes and hurried downstairs. She even waggled her fingers at the generations of dead Murrays who looked down their aristocratic noses at her as she went.

They were harmless, she decided. They might even approve of what she was doing. They, like Flynn, seemed to have been all about preserving the castle and the lands.

The kitchen was empty. The dishes were, surprisingly, already done. Daisy usually left the breakfast dishes in the sink while she cleaned in one wing of the house or another. Today the kitchen was spotless. Even Eamon's toys, usually scattered about, were neatly put away.

Sara frowned. Dishes done? Daisy gone? Dev would be at the stables. But what about Flynn and Liam?

The tree house? It was a possibility. Sara hurried back down the hall to go out into the gardens. And that was when she heard Liam's voice from the rose parlor.

The rose parlor?

He was talking in his excited voice, too—a mile a minute— but she couldn't hear what he was saying. Nor could she imagine who he was talking to.

Not Flynn, surely, unless he had decided to begin giving Liam lessons in family history. She'd never taken him in there before. The stuffiest most breakable room in the entire castle, it was reserved for state occasions—and people like Charlotte Rawsby.

Surely Flynn hadn't let Liam go in there by himself! No, of course he hadn't. Liam had to be talking to someone.

She turned the knob and pushed open the door.

And found the parlor full of people. All of them turned to stare

at her. Dev looked delighted. Liam looked happy. Flynn looked…
uncomfortable.

And the other two people—both women—looked at her as if
she'd already cleaned the chicken house before she'd come in.

The elder, an elegant woman of about sixty, had a *Town and
Country* look—all sculpted cheekbones and arched brows with
frosted graying hair in a casual cut that had no doubt cost enough
to feed a small third-world country for a week. She might as well
have had the word *countess* stamped on her forehead.

The other woman was younger and gentler looking, with a sweet
bow mouth and wavy blonde curls. She wore a twin set, tailored
slacks and pearls. She looked like a Charlotte Rawsby clone.

Oh, Lord.

Sara cringed at the thought of meeting her future mother-in-
law for the first time while she was dressed to clean the chicken
house. But at the same time she knew exactly what her own
mother would say.

"Buck up," she could hear Polly's determined tone in her ear
as if her mother were actually sitting next to her eardrum. "Unless
you've done something wrong, you have nothing to apologize for."

So she did what Polly would do. She said, "Good morning,"
as easily and cheerfully as she could.

Flynn set down his tea cup and was on his feet at once, smiling
at her. "Ah, good morning!" He took a step towards her, but
stopped abruptly, his progress halted by a tea table, his mother's
chair and that of the twin set woman.

Neither looked inclined to move.

He hesitated, then turned his attention to the countess,
"Mother, I'd like to introduce Sara—"

And Sara prepared her best meeting-mother-in-law smile.

But then Flynn stopped. She was Sara—and his mouth was
open, as if he would finish, if only he could think of what to say.

Liam, thank God, said it for him. He leapt up from where he was playing with a truck on the floor and ran across the room to throw his arms around her hips.

"My mom!" he announced proudly.

And Sara felt his solid little body with a relief that swamped her, and found herself clutching his thin shoulders as if he were her anchor in a storm.

"Ah, yes, your mother," the countess murmured. She regarded Sara over the top of her teacup. It was as effective as the Murray nose, Sara thought.

"I see," the countess said.

And Sara had no doubt that what Flynn's mother saw didn't make her happy at all.

The part of her that had squirmed yesterday when dealing with the biddies who had muttered about her being "mother of the earl's love child" wanted more than ever to turn and run today.

The part that was Polly and Lew McMaster's daughter dug in her heels and stayed right where she was.

Flynn found his voice—his earl's voice, even—at last and managed to finish his sentence. "This is Sara McMaster," he said. "My mother, the Countess of Dunmorey."

But where was his support? His declaration? His love?

Was this the same man who had made love to her so tenderly and ardently last night? The man who had built her a tree house? Who had made them a home?

Right now he looked as if he were searching for an escape route. He looked annoyed and embarrassed and out of sorts.

Welcome to the club, Sara thought irritably.

"Miss McMaster." The countess inclined her head and gave Sara a flinty smile like something you'd see on the head on an old postage stamp. It was an acknowledgment. It wasn't a welcome.

Sara smiled, too, hoping it looked more genuine. But she

was damned if she was going to curtsy. Though she did say with all the politeness she could muster, "It's a pleasure to meet you, my lady."

Was it "my lady?" Or was it "your grace?" She had no idea, and Flynn had never bothered to school her in all the aristocratic protocol.

"Don't worry," he'd said, dismissing her concerns. "You're an American. No one expects you to know that stuff."

Her lady-grace-ship certainly seemed to.

"Sara's the one who had the idea about the retreat center I was telling you about," Flynn said now and shot her a smile, though he was still trapped on the far side of the room. The countess wasn't giving an inch. "And the garden tours," he added. "And she's been helping redo the rooms."

"Came up with pony rides, too," Dev put in. He gave Sara a conspiratorial wink. "She's got a ton of good ideas."

"The restorationist." Flynn continued. "And she's been doing a lot of the manual work. The painting and wallpapering. Well you can see that, can't you?" He waved a hand around as if Sara had redone this room. She hadn't.

But the countess didn't look so sure. She let her gaze examine every inch of the parlor before it finally came to rest again on Sara.

"Did she?" Pause. "She's been very busy. She's certainly effected a great many changes around here."

Sara wasn't expecting approval by now, but she did wish that the countess would stop talking about her as if she wasn't even here.

But then, so was Flynn. "She wrote the business plan we took to the bank. Monaghan was impressed. Last time I was in he said we should make her our new business manager." The grin he gave Sara invited her to share the triumph.

Sara wasn't feeling quite so triumphant. She stared at him. Business manager?

"It's unbelievable how much she's contributed," Flynn finished. "We couldn't have done it without her."

Past tense. As if her work was done.

"Goodness," the countess said. Then at last spoke directly to Sara. "You seem to have been quite an asset to the manor."

"I've enjoyed the opportunity," Sara said politely and got for her trouble a wintery smile.

"I do hope Flynn remembered to put you on the payroll."

"Sara isn't the hired help, Mother," Flynn said sharply.

The countess looked momentarily taken aback at his vehemence. But then she simply nodded and gave him a thin smile. "Of course not, dear. She's the mother of your...child."

The pause allowed each of them their adjective of choice.

Sara began to steam. She waited for Flynn to say something—anything!—that would make her position clear.

But he only nodded curtly. "She is the mother of my child," he said firmly.

He never said she was the woman he'd spent the night with, never told his mother she was the woman he was in love with, the woman he hoped to marry.

Because, Sara realized, maybe he didn't.

He'd never even said it to her. Not since they'd been back at Dunmorey.

A deep well of cold seemed to be spreading in the pit of her stomach. She felt disoriented, dazed. Doubting now everything she'd got up this morning believing.

Maybe she was good enough to be his business manager, his bed partner, the mother of his love child, but now that Dunmorey was beginning to thrive again, perhaps he'd realized that for the rest—the society part—she didn't measure up.

God knew it was true.

She'd been completely out of her depth with the ladies at the tea yesterday. And she'd never felt so uncomfortable as she had when entertaining Charlotte Rawsby—unless you counted right this very minute.

"I hope you'll share your business plan with Abigail," the countess said now.

"Abigail?"

The countess turned a much warmer smile on the young woman seated in the rose-colored chair. "Abigail just finished a master's degree in finance. I'm sure it will be a great help."

For what?

Dear God, did the countess mean what it sounded like she meant? Was she planning on installing Abigail as lady of the manor?

As Flynn's wife?

What did Flynn think about that?

He might, she realized now, think it was a good thing. Abigail was certainly better suited than Sara was to dealing with all the pomp and circumstance that went with being the countess of Dunmorey.

If he was going to make a success of Dunmorey now—and prove once and for all that he was up to the challenge—a wife like Abigail was exactly what he would need.

"Tea?" the countess offered.

Sara nodded jerkily and took it, though a stiff shot of whiskey might have done better. It was all so "civilized."

Except it wasn't.

"I was quite surprised to meet Liam when I arrived this morning."

"Were you?" Sara said. Because Flynn hadn't told her any more than he'd told Dev about his son? She fixed Flynn with a hard accusing look.

He met it without apology.

"I've been visiting my sister in Australia," the countess said.

"Gloria and I live so far apart that we rarely get to see each other. Every few years I go out for several months or she comes here."

"How nice," Sara murmured.

"It was. I had a lovely visit. Of course I had no idea what was going on—" the countess looked around and stopped abruptly.

She didn't need to finish. Sara could fill in the blanks. Flynn's mother had had no idea what was going on here and was obviously displeased with what she found.

"Of course it was a serendipitous trip in another way," the countess went on. "I had the great good fortune to meet up with an old school chum. And Letty has lent me her most wonderful daughter." Another fond smile in the younger woman's direction. "Abigail reminds me of myself at her age."

Sara managed a polite smile. Dev seemed to choke behind his hand. Was it a laugh? Somehow, to Sara, it didn't seem especially funny.

"Abigail is an even more accomplished pianist than I was, though," the older woman went on.

"I just enjoy it," Abigail said with a self-conscious shrug and a genuine smile.

"Do you play, Miss McMaster?" the countess inquired.

It was amazing, Sara thought, how a woman could be so rude while simultaneously being perfectly polite. Polly would be laughing her head off with Dev. And Sara felt some of her mother's determined toughness settle in and take root.

"I don't," she said cheerfully. "No musical talent at all."

"Sara does a lot of other things," Flynn began in her defense, but Sara had had enough.

She wasn't going to let him waste his time trying to impress his mother any further. It was already clear what his mother's opinion was. And if all Flynn could do was defend Sara by reciting lists of things she could do, then it was clear that she didn't belong here at all.

"But my brother Jack plays the kazoo," she went on brightly. "And my sister Lizzie plays the washboard. And my other sister Daisy plays the spoons."

"Washboard? Spoons?" echoed the countess.

Even Flynn blinked at this recitation. Dev snorted. The countess, while taken aback, looked as if she felt more justified by the second.

"How...entertaining. I'm sure you're longing to see them again."

"Yes," Sara said, and the longing was growing by the minute.

"I'm sure. From what Liam tells me, you've been here awhile. How long are you planning to stay?"

"Forever," Flynn answered flatly at the same time Sara said, "We're leaving in the morning."

This time it was Flynn's teacup that rattled. He banged it down on the mantel. *"What?"*

He stared at her, stunned. But Sara knew the moment she said the words that they were the right ones. She'd been living in a fantasy if she'd thought she could live with attitudes like Flynn's mother.

"Our tickets are round trip," she said flatly. "We've been here six weeks. That's long enough."

Indeed it was, said the look on the countess's face.

The look on Flynn's face was one of fury. "No," he said.

"Flynn, you can't control everyone," his mother chided.

He shot her a furious glare. But Sara was more concerned that Liam was looking at her, stricken.

"We're going home? Tomorrow?"

Oh, God. Don't let him start to cry! "We've been on a vacation, Liam," she began in her best soothing mother tone. "We came to visit your dad, not to move in with him."

"But—"

"When we go home, you'll see Annie and Braden again. And Aunt Celie and Uncle Jace. And Grandma and Grandpa." She would have recited the whole population of Elmer or the whole state of Montana if it would make Liam remember the wonderful people he'd be going home to. "You'll like that. You can tell them all about the castle."

"And the tree house?"

The words were like a stab of pain. "And the tree house."

Liam's lip quivered. "But we just made it! I wanta stay in it. I wanta—"

"Tree house?" The countess's eyes widened. She looked from Liam to Flynn. "You built a tree house? The earl doesn't allow—"

"Mother," Flynn said, "I am the earl."

And in the shocked silence that followed, Sara picked up Liam's truck. "Come on," she said. "We'll do the chicken house. Then we have to pack."

"But—"

"It's been a pleasure to meet you," she said politely, her gaze going from Abigail to the countess. Not to mention enlightening. "Good day."

She backed out of the room, towing Liam with her, shut the door and headed for the garden. She didn't look back.

The door to her room was shut.

Flynn didn't let it stop him. If he knocked he knew she'd say, "Go away."

He shoved it open. She said it anyway.

"No, I'm not going away," he said. "And you're not, either."

But it looked like Sara thought she was. She had two suitcases open on the bed and she was pulling clothes out of the drawers of the bureau and flinging them in.

"I certainly am." She·didn't turn around, didn't even glance his way. She kept moving with the economy of controlled fury.

"Don't be so stubborn. It's all a misunderstanding," he said. "My mother didn't understand about us."

"Because you didn't bother to tell her!" More clothes came out, were flung into one of the cases.

Flynn snatched them out again and tossed them back into the drawer. "I didn't know she was coming! She showed up in the middle of breakfast. She and that…that…"

"Bridal candidate?" Sara suggested sweetly.

Flynn felt hot blood course up his neck. "Not my idea. She thought she was helping."

"Maybe she is."

"Don't be stupid. She's not."

"Perhaps she wouldn't have bothered if you'd told her you were…involved."

"But I wasn't, was I? You said no."

"Well, I shouldn't have changed my mind! And I'm changing it back again right now."

"Sara—"

"No. I made a mistake. I've made a lot of them where you're concerned, it seems. But I should have known better than to make this one. I thought it would work—"

"Damn it, it will work! My mother knows the truth now. She knows I love you. She knows you and I—"

"—are just too different." She spun around and glared at him. "She knew that very well. I didn't even know what to call her!"

Flynn frowned. "What?"

"Your mother! The countess. Or maybe she's a duchess. I don't even know! And I didn't know what to call her, either. Is she *my lady?* Is she *your grace?* I didn't have a clue! I still don't. I don't belong here!"

"Of course you belong here." He grabbed the latest armful of clothes away from her before she could put them in the suitcase. "Who brought the damned old pile to life again? Who got the bank on our side? Who got the stables finished? Who organized the nature walks? Who put the flowers in the vases?"

"I'm sure Abigail can put flowers in vases better than I can!"

"I don't want bloody Abigail! I want you!"

"Well, you can't have me."

And she grabbed the armful of clothes right back, flung them in the case, jerked down the lid and snapped it shut.

"Sara—"

She shook her head, her eyes flashing fire at him. She folded her arms across her chest. "I won't stop you having Liam. We can work out some sort of visitation. He can come for summers or something. And—" she shrugged "—we'll figure it out."

"Marry me, Sara, and we won't have to 'figure it out.'"

"No."

"You love me."

"Maybe I did. All right, maybe I do. But I'm not putting up with this. I'm not going to live in a place where I always come up short."

"What? Who said—?"

"No one had to say. I felt it. Just like you felt it. You should understand that. You and your father…you didn't want to always come up short, did you?"

She went for the jugular, he'd give her that. His mouth tightened into a firm line. He tried for his patience and clung to it. Just.

"No," he said. "I didn't."

It was suddenly quiet. So quiet he could hear his heart beat, hear her quick, shallow breathing.

She shrugged. "Well, there you are then. You want to prove

him wrong. And I don't blame you. And your mother is right. You don't need me. You need someone who can fit in. Someone who belongs. Abigail."

"I don't want Abigail, damn it! I want you."

But she only shook her head. "I'm leaving in the morning, Flynn. And there's nothing you can do or say to stop me."

"Sara—"

"You can take us to the airport if you want. If you don't, I'll call a taxi."

"You're not calling a damn taxi!"

To say that Liam wasn't happy was putting it mildly. He was stubborn, grumpy and out of sorts. He didn't want to say goodbye to Dev. He didn't want to leave the horses. He was tearful over leaving O'Mally.

"Why can't he come, then?" he asked Sara over and over.

"Because we have no room. Sid would have a fit."

Liam stuck out his lower lip. "Sid would like him. And we'd have plenty of room if we stayed. Sid could come here."

There was no arguing with him, and no reasoning with him. And Sara wasn't doing too well with reason, anyway. For a basically sane and sensible woman who valued logic and rational thought, she was a quivering jelly of emotions.

And it was all Flynn Murray's fault.

Well, maybe not all. Maybe more than a little of it was her own.

She'd just been swept up in the moment, in the challenge of saving Dunmorey, in the dream of happily ever after with the love of her life.

But just because you could refurbish a castle, make it homey and comfortable, didn't mean you ought to marry the prince.

Or the earl.

She ate dinner in her room, letting Flynn have Liam by himself for the evening. But then he had some work to do, and so she took a reluctant feet-dragging Liam around to say his goodbyes.

"Why should I?" he muttered. "It's not my idea."

"You'll be glad you did," Sara said, and knew she sounded exactly like her mother.

They went to the manor farm and said goodbye to Frank and Joe. The three boys kicked rocks and muttered at each other, then socked each other on the arm. She took him to the stables to say goodbye to the horses.

"Dev was gonna let me ride Tip Top," Liam muttered.

"You can ride Tip Top when you come to visit."

"I don't wanta visit. I wanta live here."

So did she, but it would never work. "We don't always get what we want," she said in her Polly voice.

Liam gave her a baleful look and kicked more rocks all the way home. She suggested they stop by the tree house. But he wouldn't do it.

"Why not?" She wanted to. Wanted to climb up once more and sit there and wallow in her misery. That was how much of a masochist she was.

Liam folded his arms across his chest. "Don't want to."

So Sara shrugged. "All right. It's up to you."

"If it was up to me," Liam said blackly, "we'd stay here."

As even her mother wouldn't have had a good comeback for that, Sara kept her mouth shut, too.

When they got back, the manor house was silent. Usually they all met in the yellow parlor in the evenings and talked and laughed and played with Liam and went over the projects for the next day.

Tonight the parlor was quiet when they went past. There was a light on in Flynn's study, but not a sound came out.

"I wanta see Dad," Liam said, and ran to the door.

"He might be busy," Sara warned.

But Liam pushed open the door. And Flynn, who was sitting at his desk with papers in front of him, turned, and his face lit up at the sight of his son.

"Dad!"

And Flynn opened his arms and Liam ran into them. In the hallway, Sara didn't move. But her gaze met Flynn's over the top of their son's head. Her throat was so tight she could barely swallow. His jaw worked.

"Sara—"

She turned away. "You have this time with him. Put him to bed. We need to leave at nine. I'll see you then."

And she bolted up the stairs without looking back.

At five minutes to nine she and Liam were standing in the entry hall with their luggage. O'Mally was there, looking worried. Liam was looking miserable. Dev had come through and given them both hugs.

"You'll be back," he told Liam and gave him a hard squeeze. "Or maybe I'll come and see you."

For the first time Liam looked a tiny bit eager. "When?"

Dev clearly hadn't expected to be put on the spot, but he thought a moment and said, "I could come in August."

"How long's that?" Liam asked.

"Two months."

Liam sighed at how long that was, but suggested, "And maybe you can bring O'Mally."

"Maybe," Dev agreed. He shifted awkwardly from one foot to the other, as if he wanted to leave but didn't know how.

"I'm sure you've got things to do," Sara said. "Get ready for those afternoon pony rides?" It hurt to say the words because those had been her idea.

He nodded.

She checked her watch. "Or maybe you can take us to the airport. If Flynn doesn't hurry up."

She hadn't seen him since she'd left Liam in his study last night. He wasn't there this morning. She'd seen no one at breakfast but Daisy and Eamon. She supposed the countess breakfasted in her room. Probably Abigail did, too. Flynn wasn't there, and his car wasn't out front as it usually was.

It was threatening rain. Dark clouds were pushing in. It would take them longer to get to the airport in the rain.

"He'll be here," Dev said.

But it was nine now and still no Flynn.

"How long will it take to get a taxi?" Sara asked.

"He'll come," Dev said again.

Sara tapped her foot, glanced at her watch. He wouldn't make her miss her plane, would he?

Would he?

And then, coming up the drive, she saw his car. He pulled in near where they all stood and got out. He looked resolute and grave. He wasn't smiling.

"Finally," Sara said. She wasn't smiling either. She thought she might never smile again.

"Slan leat," Dev said. "So long."

Sara knew there was an appropriate Irish response, but she couldn't think of it. Couldn't think of anything now except keeping her composure and her resolution. "Bye, Dev." Then she turned to her son. "Get in the car, Liam."

He flung himself on O'Mally and hugged the dog fiercely.

Sara couldn't watch. "Our suitcases are in the entry," she said to Flynn. "I'll get them."

But he opened the trunk of the car, then turned on his heel and disappeared into the castle. Seconds later he returned with Liam's cases and stuck them in the trunk.

"Liam. Into the car. Now."

Another fierce hug of O'Mally. Sara hoped to God she didn't have to drag Liam off him. It didn't bear thinking about.

Flynn came back with her bags and stowed them alongside Liam's. He went back into the house.

"Liam!"

His face crumpled silently, but at last he dragged himself away from the dog and climbed into the backseat. There was a child's booster seat there so he could see out. But he didn't look. He just put his hands over his face.

Flynn came out with two more suitcases and shoved them into the trunk, then turned and headed into the castle again.

Sara frowned. She looked in the trunk, then glanced at her watch, then waited until he came out with two more suitcases. "These aren't mine." She gestured towards the last two he'd put in the trunk. "And those certainly aren't." She nodded at the two he carried.

"I know that." He brushed past her and wedged them into the trunk as well, then slammed the lid. "They're mine."

She stared. Birds sang. In the meadow one of Dev's horses whinnied. Far off she could hear some farm machinery chugging away. "I— What?"

She hadn't heard him. Or if she had, didn't understand him.

"I said they're mine. I'm coming with you."

"What!" She must have shouted because all of a sudden Liam was peering at them through the backseat window.

"I said, I'm coming with you. To Montana. To Elmer. Hell, I don't care where."

Sara felt faint. Now she truly didn't understand him. "You can't."

"Of course I can. I can do what I damn well please." It was his earl's voice again. But then he said, "I threw it over. Wrote a letter. Abdicated. Resigned. Whatever the hell you want to call it. You don't want me because of the earldom, then I don't want the bloody earldom."

"Don't be ridiculous! Of course you want it. You want to prove—"

"I'm done proving. I don't have to live my life trying to prove my old man wrong. I know he's wrong. I know I'm good enough. And I don't need to be earl to prove it. I just need to be the best man I can be." He paused, met her gaze squarely with his heart in his eyes. "And I'm the best man I can be when I'm with you."

And then it was raining. Or were those tears running down her cheeks? She didn't know. Didn't care. Only cared about him.

He was standing so still, rigid almost. So rigid that she nearly knocked him right over when she threw herself at him.

"Oh, Flynn!"

And his arms went around her, clasped her hard against him, held her as if she were his lifeline—the only thing that could save him.

"Sara," he said, his voice broken, then hopeful. "Sara?"

"I'm here," she whispered, and told the truth when she said, "I'm not going anywhere."

He kissed her then—and she kissed him back. She clung to him and they held each other and rocked each other and cried and it did rain then. A few drops at first and then harder and harder.

They didn't care. They didn't notice.

They didn't notice anything until a small hopeful voice asked, "Does this mean we aren't leavin'?"

Flynn's mother was in the entry when they came back into the house. She looked at her sopping-wet son and at Sara, their arms around each other's waists, and she actually smiled.

Sara blinked at the countess, then stared at her own reflection in the mirror. It was, as usual, wet and bedraggled and small. But it was standing in the embrace of the man she loved—who loved her. Together she knew they were big enough.

"A mother's duty is to look out for her son's future and his happiness," the countess said. "You, as Liam's mother, surely understand that."

Sara nodded. That was true.

"I didn't know you at all. My son—" she shot a despairing look at Flynn "—believes face-to-face conversations are essential for imparting important news. And he did not believe he should do so in front of an outsider. Abigail," she elucidated. "Who is a lovely girl, but obviously not for him."

"There is only one woman for me," Flynn said firmly.

"So I see," his mother said, and with a real smile this time, held out a hand to Sara. "He took Abigail to the airport this morning early. It's why he was late getting back."

Sara stared, still stunned by the turn of events. But she took the countess's hand and found it warm and soft, but with calluses on her fingers. Flynn's mother smiled at Sara's surprise.

"I can get my hands dirty, too," she said. "I garden. Perhaps I can help with some of your tours—if Flynn has persuaded you to stay."

"I'm not staying," Flynn said firmly. "I told you. If they won't let Dev take the title, then the hell with it—"

"Don't say that!" Sara interrupted fiercely. "Don't. And you can't give it up."

"I have. Or I will. I—"

"No. I don't want you to."

He stared at her and shook his head. "But you didn't want—"

"I didn't want to marry a man who thought I was only Liam's mother and a good business manager. I wanted to matter."

"You always mattered! My God, Sara. What do I call you? *A stór.* My heart. I'm not alive without you. The bloody earldom—"

"Is part of who you are. And I love the man you are. And we can go back to Elmer sometimes. I love Elmer. But I love you more."

"Me, too!" Liam said. He was grinning from ear to ear, his face streaked with tears and rain, too, his arm looped over an equally grinning O'Mally.

They were married in Elmer in August. The countess—"call me Minnie" she told the wedding guests—was an enormous hit.

"Better even than when Sloan married my mom," Sara said. She was lying in bed with the man of her dreams. The wedding reception was still going on in the village hall. When they'd left, the countess was doing a square dance with Loney Bates from the welding shop. "Because everybody knew Sloan already. No mystique. Your mother has mystique."

"Not as much as you," Flynn said. He couldn't believe he'd finally got his ring on her finger. It seemed like it had taken bloody years. Well, in a sense it had. Liam was nearly six.

"She's charming them all." She giggled.

"Sara," Flynn said in his Earl's Voice.

She stopped giggling. "What?"

"I refuse to spend my honeymoon discussing my mother."

Sara pretended to consider that. "Well," she said eventually, running her bare foot up his bare leg and nuzzling his shoulder at the same time (it was wonderful to be able to multitask), "do you have any better ideas?"

He groaned. "I imagine I can think of one or two." He rolled her onto her back and began to press kisses all over her. She wiggled and giggled and then, as his mouth began to work real magic on her, she arched her back and clutched at his shoulders.

"Flynn!"

"Mmm?" He kept kissing. Teasing. Tempting. Tasting.

"Ahhh." She reached for him, drew him in, felt the completeness she only knew with Flynn.

"Mmmm." And he began to move.

"You do have good ideas," she whispered as the rhythm quickened. She moved, too, caught up with him, savored him, sheltered him, shattered him. And together, the two became one. "Very good ideas," she murmured when she could finally speak.

"I'm glad you think so." Flynn's voice was a smile against her lips. "I'll love you forever, *a stór*. And I promise I've got lots more ideas where that came from."

REQUEST YOUR FREE BOOKS!

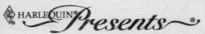 HARLEQUIN *Presents*®

 PASSION GUARANTEED SEDUCTION

2 FREE NOVELS PLUS 2 FREE GIFTS!

HP07

I ♥ HARLEQUIN Presents

BROUGHT TO YOU BY FANS OF
HARLEQUIN PRESENTS.

We are its editors and authors
and biggest fans—and we'd
love to hear from YOU!

Subscribe today to our online blog at
www.iheartpresents.com

HARLEQUIN *Presents*

He's successful, powerful—and extremely sexy....
He also happens to be her boss! Used to getting his
own way, he'll demand what he wants from her—
in the boardroom and the bedroom....

**Watch the sparks fly as these couples
work together—and play together!**

IN BED WITH
THE BOSS

The big miniseries from

HARLEQUIN® *Presents*®

Dare you read it?

Bedded by *Blackmail*

Forced to bed...then to wed?

He's got her firmly in his sights and she's got
only one chance of survival—surrender to his
blackmail...and him...in his bed!

THE ITALIAN
RAGS-TO-RICHES WIFE
by *Julia James*
Book # 2716

Laura Stowe has something Allesandro di Vincenzo wants,
and he must grit his teeth and charm her into his bed, where
she will learn the meaning of desire....

Available April 2008 wherever books are sold.

Don't miss more titles in the
BEDDED BY BLACKMAIL series—coming soon!